Christmas Eve

By

Edward Everett Hale

I.

CHRISTMAS EVE.

"

THEY'VE come! they've come!"

This was the cry of little Herbert as he ran in from the square stone which made the large doorstep of the house. Here he had been watching, a self-posted sentinel, for the moment when the carriage should turn the corner at the bottom of the hill.

"They've come! they've come!" echoed joyfully through the house; and the cry penetrated out into the extension, or ell, in which the grown members of the family were, in the kitchen, "getting tea" by some formulas more solemn than ordinary.

"Have they come?" cried Grace; and she set her skillet back to the quarter-deck, or after-part of the stove, lest its white contents should burn while she was away. She threw a waiting handkerchief over her shoulders, and ran with the others to the front door, to wave something white, and to be in at the first welcome.

Young and old were gathered there in that hospitable open space where the side road swept up to the barn on its way from the main road. The bigger boys of the home party had scattered half-way down the hill by this time. Even grandmamma had stepped down from the stone, and walked half-way to the roadway. Every one was waving something. Those who had no handkerchiefs had hats or towels to wave; and the more advanced boys began an undefined or irregular cheer.

But the carryall advanced slowly up the hill, with no answering handkerchief, and no bonneted head stretched out from the side. And, as it neared Sam and Andrew, their enthusiasm could be seen to droop, and George and Herbert stopped their cheers as it came up to them; and before it was near the house, on its grieved way up the hill, the bad news had come up before it, as bad news will,—"She has not come, after all."

It was Huldah Root, Grace's older sister, who had not come. John Root, their father, had himself driven down to the station to meet her; and Abner, her oldest brother, had gone with him. It was two years since she had been at home, and the whole family was on tiptoe to welcome her. Hence the unusual tea preparation; hence the sentinel on the doorstep; hence the general assembly in the yard; and, after all, she had not come! It was a wretched disappointment. Her mother had that heavy, silent look, which children take as the heaviest affliction of all, when they see it in their mother's faces. John Root himself led the horse into the barn, as if he did not care now for anything which might happen in heaven above or in earth beneath. The boys were voluble in their rage: "It is too bad!" and, "Grandmamma, don't you think it is too bad?" and, "It is the meanest thing I ever heard of in all my life!" and, "Grace, why don't you say anything? did you ever know anything so mean?" As for poor Grace herself, she was quite beyond saying anything. All the treasured words she had laid up to say to Huldah; all the doubts and hopes and guesses, which were secret to all but God, but which were to be poured out in Huldah's ear as soon as they were alone, were coming up one by one, as if to choke her. She had waited so long for this blessed fortnight of sympathy, and now she had lost it. Grace could say nothing. And poor grandmamma, on whom fell the stilling of the boys, was at heart as wretched as any of them.

Somehow, something got itself put on the supper-table; and, when John Root and Abner came in from the barn, they all sat down to pretend to eat something. What a miserable contrast to the Christmas eve party which had been expected!

The observance of Christmas is quite a novelty in the heart of New England among the lords of the manor. Winslow and Brewster, above Plymouth Rock, celebrated their first Christmas by making all hands work all day in the raising of their first house. It was in that way that a Christian empire was begun. They builded better than they knew. They and theirs, in that hard day's work, struck the key-note for New England for two centuries and a half. And many and many a New Englander, still in middle life, remembers that in childhood, though nurtured in Christian homes, he could not have told, if he were asked, on what day of the year Christmas fell. But as New England, in the advance of the world, has come into the general life of the world, she has shown no inaptitude for the greater enjoyments of life; and, with the true catholicity of her great Congregational system, her people and her churches seize, one after another, all the noble traditions of the loftiest memories. And so in this matter we have in hand; it happened that the Roots, in their hillside home, had determined that they would celebrate Christmas, as never had Roots done before since Josiah Root landed at Salem, from the "Hercules," with other Kentish people, in 1635. Abner and Gershom had cut and trimmed a pretty fir-balsam from the edge of the Hotchkiss clearing; and it was now in the best parlor. Grace, with Mary Bickford, her firm ally and other self, had gilded nuts, and rubbed lady apples, and strung popped corn; and the tree had been dressed in secret, the youngsters all locked and warned out from the room. The choicest turkeys of the drove, and the tenderest geese from the herd, and the plumpest fowls from the barnyard, had been sacrificed on consecrated altars. And all this was but as accompaniment and side illustration of the great glory of the celebration, which was, that Huldah, after her two years' absence,—Huldah was to come home.

And now she had not come,—nay, was not coming!

As they sat down at their Barmecide feast, how wretched the assemblage of unrivalled dainties seemed! John Root handed to his wife their daughter's letter; she read it, and gave it to Grace, who read it, and gave it to her grandmother. No one read it aloud. To read aloud in such trials is not the custom of New England.

Boston, Dec. 24, 1848.

Dear Father and Mother,—It is dreadful to disappoint you all, but I cannot come. I am all ready, and this goes by the carriage that was to take me to the cars. But our dear little Horace has just been brought home, I am afraid, dying; but we cannot tell, and I cannot leave him. You know there is really no one who can do what I can. He was riding on his pony. First the pony came home alone; and, in five minutes after, two policemen brought the dear child in a carriage. His poor mother is very calm, but cannot think yet, or do anything. We have sent for his father, who is down town. I try to hope that he may come to himself; but he only lies and draws long breaths on his little bed. The doctors are with him now; and I write this little scrawl to say how dreadfully sorry I am. A merry Christmas to you all. Do not be troubled about me.

Your own loving

HULDAH.

P.S. I have got some little presents for the children; but they are all in my trunk, and I cannot get them out now. I will make a bundle Monday. Good-by. The man is waiting.

This was the letter that was passed from hand to hand, of which the contents slowly trickled into the comprehension of all parties, according as their several ages permitted them to comprehend. Sam, as usual, broke the silence by saying,—

"It is a perfect shame! She might as well be a nigger slave! I suppose they think they have bought her and sold her. I should like to see 'em all, just for once, and tell 'em that her flesh and blood is as good as theirs; and that, with all their airs and their money, they've no business to"—

"Sam," said poor Grace, "you shall not say such things. Huldah has stayed because she chose to stay; and that is the worst of it. She will not think of herself, not for one minute; and so—everything happens."

And Grace was sobbing beyond speech again; and her intervention amounted, therefore, to little or nothing. The boys, through the evening, descanted among themselves on the outrage. Grandmamma, and at last their mother, took successive turns in taming their indignation; but, for all this, it was a miserable evening. As for John Root, he took a lamp in one hand, and "The Weekly Tribune" in the other, and sat before the fire, and pretended to read; but not once did John Root change the fold of the paper that evening. It was a wretched Christmas eve; and, at half-past eight, every light was out, and every member of the household was lying stark awake, in bed.

Huldah Root, you see, was a servant with the Bartletts, in Boston. When she was only sixteen, she was engaged at her "trade," as a vest-maker, in that town; and, by some chance, made an appointment to sew as a seamstress at Mrs. Bartlett's for a fortnight. There were any number of children to be clothed there; and the fortnight extended to a month. Then the month became two months. She grew fond of Mrs. Bartlett, because Mrs. Bartlett grew fond of her. The children adored her; and she kept an eye to them; and it ended in her engaging to spend the winter there, half-seamstress, half-nurse, half-nursery-governess, and a little of everything. From such a beginning, it had happened that she had lived there six years, in confidential service. She could cook better than anybody in the house,— better than Mrs. Bartlett herself; but it was not often that she tried her talent there. On a birthday perhaps, in August, she would make huckleberry cakes, by the old homestead "receipt," for the children. She had the run of all their clothes as nobody else did; took the younger ones to be measured; and saw that none of the older ones went out with a crack in a seam, or a rough edge at the foot of a trowser. It was whispered that Minnie had rather go into the sewing-room to get Huldah to "show her" about "alligation" or "square-root," than to wait for Miss Thurber's explanations in the morning. In fifty such ways, it happened that Huldah—who, on the roll-call of the census-man, probably rated as a nursery-maid in the house—was the confidential friend of every member of the family, from Mr. Bartlett, who wanted to know where "The Intelligencer" was, down to the chore-boy who came in to black the shoes. And so it was, that, when poor little Horace was brought in with his skull knocked in by the pony, Huldah was—and modestly knew that she was—the most essential person in the stunned family circle.

While her brothers and sisters were putting out their lights at New Durham, heart-sick and wounded, Huldah was sitting in that still room, where only the rough broken breathing of poor Horace broke the sound. She was changing, once in ten minutes, the ice-water cloths; was feeling of his feet sometimes; wetting his tongue once or twice in an hour; putting her finger to his pulse with a native sense, which needed no second-hand to help it; and all the time, with the thought of him, was remembering how grieved and hurt and heart-broken they were at home. Every half-hour or less, a pale face appeared at the door; and Huldah just slid across the room, and said, "He is really doing nicely, pray lie down;" or, "His pulse is surely better, I will certainly come to you if it flags;" or "Pray trust me, I will not let you wait a moment if he needs you;" or, "Pray get ready for to-morrow. An hour's sleep now will be worth everything to you then." And the poor mother would crawl back to her baby and her bed, and pretend to try to sleep; and in half an hour would appear again at the door. One o'clock, two o'clock, three o'clock. How companionable Dr. Lowell's clock seems when one is sitting up so, with no one else to talk to! Four o'clock at last; it is really growing to be quite intimate. Five o'clock. "If I were in dear Durham now, one of the roosters would be calling,"—Six o'clock. Poor Horace stirs, turns, flings his arm over. "Mother—O Huldah! is it you? How nice that is!" And he is unconscious again; but he had had sense enough to know her. What a blessed Christmas present that is, to tell that to his poor mother when she slides in at daybreak, and says, "You shall go to bed now, dear child. You see I am very fresh; and you must rest yourself, you know. Do you really say he knew you? Are you sure he knew you? Why, Huldah, what an angel of peace you are!"

So opened Huldah's Christmas morning.

Days of doubt, nights of watching. Every now and then the boy knows his mother, his father, or Huldah. Then will come this heavy stupor which is so different from sleep. At last the surgeons have determined that a piece of the bone must come away. There is the quiet gathering of the most skilful at the determined hour; there is the firm table for the little fellow to lie on; here is the ether and the sponge; and, of course, here and there, and everywhere, is Huldah. She can hold the sponge, or she can fetch and carry; she can answer at once if she is spoken to; she can wait, if it is waiting; she can act, if it is acting. At last the wretched little button, which has been pressing on our poor boy's brain, is lifted safely out. It is in Morton's hand; he smiles and nods at Huldah as she looks inquiry, and she knows he is satisfied. And does not the poor child himself, even in his unconscious sleep, draw his breath more lightly than he did before? All is well.

"Who do you say that young woman is?" says Dr. Morton to Mr. Bartlett, as he draws on his coat in the doorway after all is over. "Could we not tempt her over to the General Hospital?"

"No, I think not. I do not think we can spare her."

The boy Horace is new-born that day; a New Year's gift to his mother. So pass Huldah's holidays.

II.

CHRISTMAS AGAIN.

FOURTEEN years make of the boy whose pony has been too much for him a man equal to any prank of any pony. Fourteen years will do this, even to boys of ten. Horace Bartlett is the colonel of a cavalry regiment, stationed just now in West Virginia; and, as it happens, this twenty-four-year-old boy has an older commission than anybody in that region, and is the Post Commander at Talbot C. H., and will be, most likely, for the winter. The boy has a vein of foresight in him; a good deal of system; and, what is worth while to have by the side of system, some knack of order. So soon as he finds that he is responsible, he begins to prepare for responsibility. His staff-officers are boys too; but they are all friends, and all mean to do their best. His Surgeon-in-Charge took his degree at Washington last spring; that is encouraging. Perhaps, if he has not much experience, he has, at least, the latest advices. His head is level too; he means to do his best, such as it is; and, indeed, all hands in that knot of boy counsellors will not fail for laziness or carelessness. Their very youth makes them provident and grave.

So among a hundred other letters, as October opens, Horace writes this:—

TALBOT COURT HOUSE, VA.,
Oct. 3, 1863.

DEAR HULDAH,—Here we are still, as I have been explaining to father; and, as you will see by my letter to him, here we are like to stay. Thus far we are doing sufficiently well. As I have told him, if my plans had been adopted we should have been pushed rapidly forward up the valley of the Yellow Creek; Badger's corps would have been withdrawn from before Winchester; Wilcox and Steele together would have threatened Early; and then, by a rapid flank movement, we should have pounced down on

Longstreet (not the great Longstreet, but little Longstreet), and compelled him to uncover Lynchburg; we could have blown up the dams and locks on the canal, made a freshet to sweep all the obstructions out of James River, and then, if they had shown half as much spirit on the Potomac, all of us would be in Richmond for our Christmas dinner. But my plans, as usual, were not asked for, far less taken. So, as I said, here we are.

Well, I have been talking with Lawrence Worster, my Surgeon-in-Charge, who is a very good fellow. His sick-list is not bad now, and he does not mean to have it bad; but he says that he is not pleased with the ways of his ward-masters; and it was his suggestion, not mine, mark you, that I should see if one or two of the Sanitary women would not come as far as this to make things decent. So, of course, I write to you. Don't you think mother could spare you to spend the winter here? It will be rough, of course; but it is all in the good cause. Perhaps you know some nice women,—well, not like you, of course; but still, disinterested and sensible, who would come too. Think of this carefully, I beg you, and talk to father and mother. Worster says we may have three hundred boys in hospital before Christmas. If Jubal Early should come this way, I don't know how many more. Talk with mother and father.

Always yours,

Horace Bartlett.

P. S. I have shown Worster what I have written; he encloses a sort of official letter which may be of use. He says, "Show this to Dr. Hayward; get them to examine you and the others, and then the government, on his order, will pass you on." I enclose this, because, if you come, it will save time.

Of course Huldah went. Grace Starr, her married sister, went with her, and Mrs. Philbrick, and Anna Thwart. That was the way they happened to be all together in the Methodist Church that had been, of Talbot Court House, as Christmas holidays drew near, of the year of grace, 1863.

She and her friends had been there quite long enough to be wonted to the strangeness of December in the open air. On her little table in front of the desk of the church were three or four buttercups in bloom, which she had gathered in an afternoon walk, with three or four heads of hawksweed. "The beginning of one year," Huldah said, "with the end of the other." Nay, there was even a stray rose which Dr. Sprigg had found in a farmer's garden. Huldah came out from the vestry, where her own bed was, in the gray of the morning, changed the water for the poor little flowers, sat a moment at the table to look at last night's memoranda, and then beckoned to the ward-master, and asked him, in a whisper, what was the movement she had heard in the night,—"Another alarm from Early?"

"No, Miss; not an alarm. I saw the Colonel's orderly as he passed. He stopped here for Dr. Fenno's case. There had come down an express from General Mitchell, and the men were called without the bugle, each man separately; not a horse was to neigh, if they could help it. And really, Miss, they were off in twenty minutes."

"Off, who are off?"

"The whole post, Miss, except the relief for to-day. There are not fifty men in the village besides us here. The orderly thought they were to go down to Braxton's; but he did not know."

Here was news indeed! news so exciting that Huldah went back at once, and called the other women; and then all of them together began on that wretched business of waiting. They had never yet known what it was to wait for a real battle. They had had their beds filled with this and that patient from one or another post, and had some gun-shot wounds of old standing among the rest; but this was their first battle if it were a battle. So the covers were taken off that long line of beds, down on the west aisle, and from those under the singers' seat; and the sheets and pillow-cases were brought out from the linen room, and aired, and put on. Our biggest kettles are filled up with strong soup; and we have our milk-punch, and our beef-tea all in readiness; and everybody we can command is on hand to help lift patients and distribute food. But there is only too much time. Will there never be any news? Anna Thwart and Doctor Sprigg have walked down to the bend of the hill, to see if any messenger is coming. As for the other women, they sit at their table; they look at their watches; they walk down to the door; they come back to the table. I notice they have all put on fresh aprons, for the sake of doing something more in getting ready.

Here is Anna Thwart. "They are coming! they are coming! somebody is coming. A mounted man is crossing the flat, coming towards us; and the doctor told me to come back and tell." Five minutes more, ten minutes more, an eternity more, and then, rat-tat-tat, rat-tat-tat, the mounted man is here. "Wagons right behind. We bagged every man of them at Wyatt's. Got there before daylight. Colonel White's men from the Yellows came up just at the same time, and we pitched in before they knew it,—three or four regiments, thirteen hundred men, and all their guns."

"And with no fighting?"

"Oh, yes! fighting of course. The colonel has got a train of wagons down here with the men that are hurt. That's why I am here. Here is his note." Thus does the mounted man discharge his errand backward.

Dear Doctor,—We have had great success. We have surprised the whole post. The company across the brook tried hard to get away; and a good many of them, and of Sykes's men, are hit; but I cannot find that we have lost more than seven men. I have nineteen wagons here of wounded men,— some hurt pretty badly.

Ever yours, H.

So there must be more waiting. But now we know what we are waiting for; and the end will come in a finite world. Thank God, at half-past three, here they are! Tenderly, gently. "Hush, Sam! Hush, Cæsar! You talk too much." Gently, tenderly. Twenty-seven of the poor fellows, with everything the matter, from a burnt face to a heart stopping its beats for want of more blood.

"Huldah, come here. This is my old classmate, Barthow; sat next me at prayers four years. He is a major in their army, you see. His horse stumbled, and pitched him against a stone wall; and he has not spoken since. Don't tell me he is dying; but do as well for him, Huldah,"—and the handsome boy smiled,—"do as well for him as you did for me." So they carried Barthow, senseless as he was, tenderly into the church; and he became E, 27, on an iron bedstead. Not half our soup was wanted, nor our beef-tea, nor our punch. So much the better.

Then came day and night, week in and out, of army system, and womanly sensibility; that quiet, cheerful, *homish*, hospital life, in the quaint surroundings of the white-washed church; the pointed arches of the windows and the faded moreen of the pulpit telling that it is a church, in a reminder not unpleasant. Two or three weeks of hopes and fears, failures and success, bring us to Christmas eve.

It is the surgeon-in-chief, who happens to give our particular Christmas dinner,—I mean the one that interests you and me. Huldah and the other ladies had accepted his invitation. Horace Bartlett and his staff, and some of the other officers, were guests; and the doctor had given his own permit that Major Barthow might walk up to his quarters with the ladies. Huldah and he were in advance, he leaning, with many apologies, on her arm. Dr. Sprigg and Anna Thwart were far behind. The two married ladies, as needing no escort, were in the middle. Major Barthow enjoyed the emancipation, was delighted with his companion, could not say enough to make her praise the glimpses of Virginia, even if it were West Virginia.

"What a party it is, to be sure!" said he. "The doctor might call on us for our stories, as one of Dickens's chiefs would do at a Christmas feast. Let's see, we should have

THE SURGEON'S TALE;
THE GENERAL'S TALE;

for we may at least make believe that Hod's stars have come from Washington. Then we must call in that one-eyed servant of his; and we will have

THE ORDERLY'S TALE.

Your handsome friend from Wisconsin shall tell

THE GERMAN'S TALE.

I shall be encouraged to tell

THE PRISONER'S TALE.

And you"—

"And I?" said Huldah laughing, because he paused.

"You shall tell

THE SAINT'S TALE."

Barthow spoke with real feeling, which he did not care to disguise. But Huldah was not there for sentiment; and without quivering in the least, nor making other acknowledgment, she laughed as she knew she ought to do, and said, "Oh, no! that is quite too grand, the story must end with

THE SUPERINTENDENT OF SPECIAL RELIEF'S TALE.

It is a little unromantic to the sound; but that's what it is."

"I don't see," persisted the major, "if Superintendent of Special Relief means Saint in Latin, why we should not say so."

"Because we are not talking Latin," said Huldah. "Listen to me; and, before we come to dinner, I will tell you a story pretty enough for Dickens, or any of them; and it is a story not fifteen minutes old.

"Have you noticed that black-whiskered fellow, under the gallery, by the north window?—Yes, the same. He is French, enlisted, I think, in New London. I came to him just now, managed to say *étrennes* and *Noël* to him, and a few other French words, and asked if there were nothing we could do to make him more at home. Oh, no! there was nothing; madame was too good, and everybody was too good, and so on. But I persisted. I wished I knew more about Christmas in France; and I staid by. 'No, madame, nothing; there is nothing. But, since you say it,—if there were two drops of red wine,—*du vin de mon pays, madame*; but you could not here in Virginia.' Could not I? A superintendent of special relief has long arms. There was a box of claret, which was the first thing I saw in the store-room the day I took my keys. The doctor was only too glad the man had thought of it; and you should have seen the pleasure that red glass, as full as I could pile it, gave him. The tears were running down his cheeks. Anna, there, had another Frenchman; and she sent some to him: and my man is now humming a little song about the *vin rouge* of Bourgogne. Would not Mr. Dickens make a pretty story of that for you,—'THE FRENCHMAN'S STORY'?"

Barthow longed to say that the great novelist would not make so pretty a story as she did. But this time he did not dare.

You are not going to hear the eight stories. Mr. Dickens was not there; nor, indeed, was I. But a jolly Christmas dinner they had; though they had not those eight stories. Quiet they were, and very, very happy. It was a strange thing,—if one could have analyzed it,—that they should have felt so much at home, and so much at ease with each other, in that queer Virginian kitchen, where the doctor and his friends of his mess had arranged the feast. It was a happy thing, that the recollections of so many other Christmas homes should come in, not sadly, but pleasantly, and should cheer, rather than shade the evening. They felt off soundings, all of them. There was, for the time, no responsibility. The strain was gone. The gentlemen were glad to be dining with ladies, I believe: the ladies, unconsciously, were probably glad to be dining with gentlemen. The officers were glad they were not on duty; and the prisoner, if glad of nothing else, was glad he was not in bed. But he was glad for many things beside. You see it was but a little post. They were far away; and they took things with the ease of a detached command.

"Shall we have any toasts?" said the doctor, when his nuts and raisins and apples at last appeared.

"Oh, no! no toasts,—nothing so stiff as that."

"Oh, yes! oh, yes!" said Grace. "I should like to know what it is to drink a toast. Something I have heard of all my life, and never saw."

"One toast, at least, then," said the doctor. "Colonel Bartlett, will you name the toast?"

"Only one toast?" said Horace; "that is a hard selection: we must vote on that."

"No, no!" said a dozen voices; and a dozen laughing assistants at the feast offered their advice.

"I might give 'The Country;' I might give 'The Cause;' I might give 'The President:' and everybody would drink," said Horace. "I might give 'Absent friends,' or 'Home, sweet home;' but then we should cry."

"Why do you not give 'The trepanned people'?" said Worster, laughing, "or 'The silver-headed gentlemen'?"

"Why don't you give 'The Staff and the Line'?" "Why don't you give 'Here's Hoping'?" "Give 'Next Christmas.'" "Give 'The Medical Department; and may they often ask us to dine!'"

"Give 'Saints and Sinners,'" said Major Barthow, after the first outcry was hushed.

"I shall give no such thing," said Horace. "We have had a lovely dinner; and we know we have; and the host, who is a good fellow, knows the first thanks are not to him. Those of us who ever had our heads knocked open, like the Major and me, do know. Fill your glasses, gentlemen; I give you 'the Special Diet Kitchen.'"

He took them all by surprise. There was a general shout; and the ladies all rose, and dropped mock courtesies.

"By Jove!" said Barthow to the Colonel, afterwards, "It was the best toast I ever drank in my life. Anyway, that little woman has saved my life. Do you say she did the same to you?"

III.

CHRISTMAS AGAIN.

So you think that when the war was over Major Barthow, then Major-General, remembered Huldah all the same, and came on and persuaded her to marry him, and that she is now sitting in her veranda, looking down on the Pamunkey River. You think that, do not you?

Well! you were never so mistaken in your life. If you want that story, you can go and buy yourself a dime novel. I would buy "The Rescued Rebel;" or, "The Noble Nurse," if I were you.

After the war was over, Huldah did make Colonel Barthow and his wife a visit once, at their plantation in Pocataligo County; but I was not there, and know nothing about it.

Here is a Christmas of hers, about which she wrote a letter; and, as it happens, it was a letter to Mrs. Barthow.

HULDAH ROOT TO AGNES BARTHOW.

VILLERS-BOCAGE, Dec. 27, 1868.

... Here I was, then, after this series of hopeless blunders, sole alone at the *gare* [French for station] of this little out-of-the-way town. My dear, there was never an American here since Christopher Columbus slept here when he was a boy. And here, you see, I was like to remain; for there was no possibility of the others getting back to me till to-morrow, and no good in my trying to overtake them. All I could do was just to bear it, and live on, and live through from Thursday to Monday; and, really, what was worst of all was that Friday was Christmas day.

Well, I found a funny little carriage, with a funny old man who did not understand my *patois* any better than I did his; but he understood a franc-piece. I had my guide-book, and I said *auberge*; and we came to the oddest, most outlandish, and old-fashioned establishment that ever escaped from one of Julia Nathalie woman's novels. And here I am.

And the reason, my dear Mrs. Barthow, that I take to-day to write to you, you and the Colonel will now understand. You see it was only ten o'clock when I got here; then I went to walk, many *enfans terribles* following respectfully; then I came home, and ate the funny refection; then I got a nap; then I went to walk again, and made a little sketch in the churchyard: and this time, one of the children brought up her mother, a funny Norman woman, in a delicious costume,—I have a sketch of another just like her,—and she dropped a courtesy, and in a very mild *patois* said she hoped the children did not trouble madame. And I said, "Oh, no!" and found a sugar-plum for the child and showed my sketch to the woman; and she said she supposed madame was *Anglaise*.

I said I was not *Anglaise*,—and here the story begins; for I said I was *Americaine*. And, do you know, her face lighted up as if I had said I was St. Gulda, or St. Hilda, or any of their Northmen Saints.

"Americaine! est-il possible? Jeannette, Gertrude, faites vos révérences. Madame est Americaine."

And, sure enough, they all dropped preternatural courtesies. And then the most eager enthusiasm; how fond they all were of *les Americaines*, but how no *Americaines* had ever come before! And was madame at the Three Cygnets? And might she and her son and her husband call to see madame at the Three Cygnets? And might she bring a little *étrenne* to madame? And I know not what beside.

I was very glad the national reputation had gone so far. I really wished I were Charles Sumner (pardon me, dear Agnes), that I might properly receive the delegation. But I said, "Oh, certainly!" and, as it grew dark, with my admiring *cortége* whispering now to the street full of admirers that madame was *Americaine,* I returned to the Three Cygnets.

And in the evening they all came. Really, you should see the pretty basket they brought for an *étrenne.* I could not guess then where they got such exquisite flowers; these lovely stephanotis blossoms, a perfect wealth of roses, and all arranged with charming taste in a quaint country basket, such as exists nowhere but in this particular section of this quaint old Normandy. In came the husband, dressed up, and frightened, but thoroughly good in his look. In came my friend; and then two sons and two wives, and three or four children: and, my dear Agnes, one of the sons, I knew him in an instant, was a man we had at Talbot Court House when your husband was there. I think the Colonel will remember him,—a black-whiskered man, who used to sing a little song about *le vin rouge* of Bourgogne.

He did not remember me; that I saw in a moment. It was all so different, you know. In the hospital, I had on my cap and apron, and here,—well, it was another thing. My hostess knew that they were coming, and had me in her largest room, and I succeeded in making them all sit down; and I received my formal welcome; and I thanked in my most Parisian French; and then the conversation hung fire. But I took my turn now, and turned round to poor Louis.

"You served in America, did you not?" said I.

"Ah, yes, madame! I did not know my mother had told you."

No more did she, indeed; and she looked astonished. But I persevered,—

"You seem strong and well."

"Ah, yes, madame!"

"How long since you returned?"

"As soon as there was peace, madame. We were mustered out in June, madame."

"And does your arm never trouble you?"

"Oh, never, madame! I did not know my mother had told you."

New astonishment on the part of the mother.

"You never had another piece of bone come out?"

"Oh, no, madame! how did madame know? I did not know my mother had told you!"

And by this time I could not help saying, "You Normans care more for Christmas than we Americans; is it not so, my brave?"

And this he would not stand; and he said stoutly, "Ah, no, madame! no, no, *jamais*!" and began an eager defence of the religious enthusiasm of the Americans, and their goodness to all people who were good, if people would only be good. But still he had not the least dream who I was. And I said,—

"Do the Normans ever drink Burgundy?" and to my old hostess, "Madame, could you bring us a flask *du vin rouge de Bourgogne*?" and then I hummed his little chanson, I am sure Colonel Barthow will remember it, —"*Deux—gouttes—du vin rouge du Bourgogne.*"

My dear Mrs. Barthow, he sprang from his chair, and fell on his knees, and kissed my hands, before I could stop him. And when his mother and father, and all the rest, found that I was the particular *sœur de la charité* who had had the care of dear Louis when he was hurt, and that it was I he had told of that very day,—for the thousandth time, I believe,—who gave him that glass of claret, and cheered up his Christmas, I verily believe they would have taken me to the church to worship me. They were not satisfied, —the women with kissing me, or the men with shaking hands with each other,—the whole *auberge* had to be called in; and poor I was famous. I need not say I cried my eyes out; and when, at ten o'clock, they let me go to bed, I was worn out with crying, and laughing, and talking, and listening; and I believe they were as much upset as I.

Now that is just the beginning; and yet I see I must stop. But, for forty-eight hours, I have been simply a queen. I can hardly put my foot to the ground. Christmas morning, these dear Thibault people came again; and then the *curé* came; and then some nice Madame Perrons came, and I went to mass with them; and, after mass, their brother's carriage came; and they would take no refusals; but with many apologies to my sweet old hostess, at the Three Cygnets, I was fain to come up to M. Firmin's lovely *château* here, and make myself at home till my friends shall arrive. It seems the poor Thibaults had come here to beg the flowers for the *étrenne*. It is really the most beautiful country residence I have seen in France; and they live on the most patriarchal footing with all the people round them. I am sure I ought to speak kindly of them. It is the most fascinating hospitality. So here am I, waiting, with my little *sac de nuit* to make me *aspettabile*; and here I ate my Christmas dinner. Tell the Colonel that here is "THE TRAVELLER'S TALE;" and that is why the letter is so long.

Most truly yours,

HULDAH ROOT.

IV.

ONE CHRISTMAS MORE.

THIS last Christmas party is Huldah's own. It is hers, at least, as much as it is any one's. There are five of them, nay, six, with equal right to precedence in the John o' Groat's house, where she has settled down. It is one of those comfortable houses which are still left three miles out from the old State House in Boston. It is not all on one floor; that would be, perhaps, too much like the golden courts of heaven. There are two stories; but they are connected by a central flight of stairs of easy tread (designed by Charles Cummings); so easy, and so stately withal, that, as you pass over them, you always bless the builder, and hardly know that you go up or down. Five large rooms on each floor give ample room for the five heads of the house, if, indeed, there be not six, as I said before.

Into this Saints' Rest, there have drifted together, by the eternal law of attraction,—Huldah, and Ellen Philbrick (who was with her in Virginia, and in France, and has been, indeed, but little separated from her, except on duty, for twenty years), and with them three other friends. These women,—well, I cannot introduce them to you without writing three stories of true romance, one for each. This quiet, strong, meditative, helpful saint, who is coming into the parlor now, is Helen Touro. She was left alone with her baby when "The Empire State" went down; and her husband was never heard of more. The love of that baby warmed her to the love of all others; and, when I first knew her, she was ruling over a home of babies, whose own mothers or fathers were not,—always with a heart big enough to say there was room for one more waif in that sanctuary. That older woman, who is writing at the Davenport in the corner, lightened the cares and smoothed the daily life of General Schuyler in all the last years of his life, when he was in the Cabinet, in Brazil, and in Louisiana. His wife was long ill, and then died. His children needed all a woman's care; and this woman stepped to the front, cared for them, cared for all his household, cared for him: and I dare not say how much is due to her of that which you and I say daily we owe to him. Miss Peters, I see you know. She served in another regiment; was at the head of the sweetest, noblest, purest school that ever trained, in five and twenty years, five hundred girls to be the queens in five hundred happy and strong families. All of these five,—our Huldah and Mrs. Philbrick too, you have seen before,—all of them have been in "the service;" all of them have known that perfect service is perfect freedom. I think they know that perfect service is the highest honor. They have together taken this house, as they say, for the shelter and home of their old age. But Huldah, as she plays with your Harry there, does not look to me as if she were superannuated yet.

"But you said there were six in all."

Did I? I suppose there are. "Mrs. Philbrick, are there five captains in your establishment, or six?"

"My dear Mr. Hale, why do you ask me? You know there are five captains and one general. We have persuaded Seth Corbet to make his home here,—yes, the same who went round the world with Mrs. Cradock. Since her death, he has come home to Boston; and he reports to us, and makes his head-quarters here. He sees that we are all right every morning; and then he goes his rounds to see every grandchild of old Mr. Cradock, and to make sure that every son and daughter of that house is 'all right.' Sometimes he is away over night. This is when somebody in the whole circle of all their friends is more sick than usual, and needs a man nurse. That old man was employed by old Mr. Cradock, in 1816, when he first went to housekeeping. He has had all the sons and all the daughters of that house in his arms; and now that the youngest of them is five and twenty, and the oldest fifty, I suppose he is not satisfied any day until he has seen that they and theirs, in their respective homes, are well. He thinks we here are babies; but he takes care of us all the more courteously."

"Will he dine with you to-day?"

"I am afraid not; but we shall see him at the Christmas-tree after dinner. There is to be a tree."

You see, this house was dedicated to the Apotheosis of Noble Ministry. Over the mantel-piece hung Raphael Morghen's large print of "The Lavatio," Caracci's picture of "The Washing of the Feet,"—the only copy I ever saw. We asked Huldah about it.

"Oh, that was a present from Mr. Burchstadt, a rich manufacturer in Würtemberg, to Ellen. She stumbled into one of those villages when everybody was sick and dying of typhus, and tended and watched and saved, one whole summer long, as Mrs. Ware did at Osmotherly. And this Mr. Burchstadt wanted to do something, and he sent her this in acknowledgment."

On the other side was Kaulbach's own study of Elizabeth of Hungary, dropping her apron full of roses.

"Oh! what a sight the apron discloses;
The viands are changed to real roses!"

When I asked Huldah where that came from, she blushed, and said, "Oh, that was a present to me!" and led us to Steinler's exquisite "Good Shepherd," in a larger and finer print than I had ever seen. Six or eight gentlemen in New York, who, when they were dirty babies from the gutter, had been in Helen Touro's hands, had sent her a portfolio of beautiful prints, each with this same idea, of seeking what was lost. This one she had chosen for the sitting-room.

And, on the fourth side, was that dashing group of Horace Vernet's, "Gideon crossing Jordan," with the motto wrought into the frame, "Faint, yet pursuing." These four pictures are all presents to the "girls," as I find I still call them; and, on the easel, Miss Peters had put her copy of "The Tribute Money." There were other pictures in the room; but these five unconsciously told its story.

The five "girls" were always all together at Christmas; but, in practice, each of them lived here only two-fifths of her time. "We make that a rule," said Ellen laughing. "If anybody comes for anybody when there are only two here, those two are engaged to each other; and we stay. Not but what they can come and stay here if we cannot go to them." In practice, if any of us in the immense circles which these saints had befriended were in a scrape,—as, if a mother was called away from home, and there were some children left, or if scarlet fever got into a house, or if the children had nobody to go to Mt. Desert with them, or if the new house were to be set in order, and nobody knew how,—in any of the trials of well-ordered families, why, we rode over to the Saints' Rest to see if we could not induce one of the five to come and put things through. So that, in practice, there were seldom more than two on the spot there.

But we do not get to the Christmas dinner. There were covers for four and twenty; and all the children besides were in a room upstairs, presided over by Maria Munro, who was in her element there. Then our party of twenty-four included men and women of a thousand romances, who had learned and had shown the nobility of service. One or two of us were invited as novices, in the hope perhaps that we might learn.

Scarcely was the soup served when the door-bell rang. Nothing else ever made Huldah look nervous. Bartlett, who was there, said in an aside to me, that he had seen her more calm when there was volley firing within hearing of her store-room. Then it rang again. Helen Touro talked more vehemently; and Mrs. Bartlett at her end, started a great laugh. But, when it rang the third time, something had to be said; and Huldah asked one of the girls, who was waiting, if there were no one attending at the door.

"Yes 'm, Mr. Corbet."

But the bell rang a fourth time, and a fifth.

"Isabel, you can go to the door. Mr. Corbet must have stepped out."

So Isabel went out, but returned with a face as broad as a soup-plate. "Mr. Corbet is there, ma'am."

Sixth door-bell peal,—seventh, and eighth.

"Mary, I think you had better see if Mr. Corbet has gone away."

Mary returns, face one broad grin.

"No, ma'am, Mr. Corbet is there."

Heavy steps in the red parlor. Side door-bell—a little gong, begins to ring. Front bell rings ninth time, tenth, and eleventh.

Saint John, as we call him, had seen that something was amiss, and had kindly pitched in with a dissertation on the passage of the Red-River Dam, in which the gravy-boats were steamships, and the cranberry was General Banks, and the aids were spoons. But, when both door-bells rang together, and there were more steps in the hall, Huldah said, "If you will excuse me," and rose from the table.

"No, no, we will not excuse you," cried Clara Hastings. "Nobody will excuse you. This is the one day of the year when you are not to work. Let me go." So Clara went out. And after Clara went out, the door-bells rang no more. I think she cut the bell-wires. She soon came back, and said a man was inquiring his way to the "Smells;" and they directed him to "Wait's Mills," which she hoped would do. And so Huldah's and Grace's stupendous housekeeping went on in its solid order, reminding one of those well-proportioned Worcester teas which are, perhaps, the crown and glory of the New England science in this matter. I ventured to ask Sam Root, who sat by me, if the Marlborough were not equal to his mother's.

And we sat long; and we laughed loud. We talked war and poetry and genealogy. We rallied Helen Touro about her housekeeping; and Dr. Worster pretended to give a list of Surgeons and Majors and Major-Generals who had made love to Huldah. By and by, when the grapes and the bonbons came, the sixteen children were led in by Maria Munro, who had, till now, kept them at games of string and hunt the slipper. And, at last, Seth Corbet flung open the door into the red parlor to announce "The Tree."

Sure enough, there was the tree, as the five saints had prepared it for the invited children,—glorious in gold, and white with wreaths of snow-flakes, and blazing with candles. Sam Root kissed Grace, and said, "O Grace! do you remember?" But the tree itself did not surprise the children as much as the five tables at the right and the left, behind and before, amazed the Sainted Five, who were indeed the children now. A box of the *vin rouge de Bourgogne*, from Louis, was the first thing my eye lighted on, and above it a little banner read, "Huldah's table." And then I saw that there were these five tables, heaped with the Christmas offerings to the five saints. It proved that everybody, the world over, had heard that they had settled down. Everybody in the four hemispheres,—if there be four,—who had remembered the unselfish service of these five, had thought this a fit time for commemorating such unselfish love, were it only by such a present as a lump of coal. Almost everybody, I think, had made Seth Corbet a confidant; and so, while the five saints were planning their pretty tree for the sixteen children, the North and the South, and the East and the West, were sending myrrh and frankincense and gold to them. The pictures were hung with Southern moss from Barthow. Boys, who were now men, had sent coral from India, pearl from Ceylon, and would have been glad to send ice from Greenland, had Christmas come in midsummer; there were diamonds from Brazil, and silver from Nevada, from those who lived there; there were books, in the choicest binding, in memory of copies of the same word, worn by travel, or dabbled in blood; there were pictures, either by the hand of near friendship, or by the master hand of genius, which brought back the memories, perhaps, of some old adventure in "The Service,"—perhaps, as the Kaulbach did, of one of those histories which makes all service sacred. In five and twenty years of life, these women had so surrounded themselves, without knowing it or thinking of it, with loyal, yes, adoring friends, that the accident of their finding a fixed home had called in all at once this wealth of acknowledgment from those whom they might have forgotten, but who would never forget them. And, by the accident of our coming together, we saw, in these heaps on heaps of offerings of love, some faint record of the lives they had enlivened, the wounds they had stanched, the tears they had wiped away, and the homes they had cheered. For themselves, the five saints—as I have called them—were laughing and crying together, quite upset in the surprise. For ourselves, there was not one of us who, in this little visible display of the range of years of service, did not take in something more of the meaning of,—

"He who will be chief among you, let him be your servant."

The surprise, the excitement, the laughter, and the tears found vent in the children's eagerness to be led to their tree; and, in three minutes, Ellen was opening boxes, and Huldah pulling fire-crackers, as if they had not been thrown off their balance. But, when each boy and girl had two arms full, and the fir balsam sent down from New Durham was nearly bare, Edgar Bartlett pointed to the top bough, where was a brilliant not noticed before. No one had noticed it,—not Seth himself,—who had most of the other secrets of that house in his possession. I am sure that no man, woman, or child knew how the thing came there: but Seth lifted the little discoverer high in air, and he brought it down triumphant. It was a parcel made up in shining silvered paper. Seth cut the strings.

It contained twelve Maltese crosses of gold, with as many jewels, one in the heart of each,—I think the blazing twelve of the Revelations. They were displayed on ribbons of blue and white, six of which bore Huldah's, Helen's, Ellen Philbrick's, Hannah's, Miss Peters's, and Seth Corbet's names. The other six had no names; but on the gold of these was marked,—"From Huldah, to ——" "From Helen, to ——-" and so on, as if these were decorations which they were to pass along. The saints themselves were the last to understand the decorations; but the rest of us caught the idea, and pinned them on their breasts. As we did so, the ribbons unfolded, and displayed the motto of the order:—

"Henceforth I call you not servants, I have called you friends."

It was at that Christmas that the "Order of Loving Service" was born.

THE TWO PRINCES.

A STORY FOR CHILDREN.

I.

THERE was a King of Hungary whose name was Adelbert.

When he lived at home, which was not often, it was in a castle of many towers and many halls and many stairways, in the city of Buda, by the side of the river Donau.

He had four daughters, and only one son, who was to be the King after him, whose name was Ladislaus. But it was the custom of those times, as boys and girls grew up, to send them for their training to some distance from their home, even for many months at a time, to try a little experiment on them, and see how they fared; and so, at the time I tell you of, there was staying in the castle of Buda the Prince Bela, who was the son of the King of Bohemia; and he and the boy Ladislaus studied their lessons together, and flew their kites, and hunted for otters, and rode with the falconers together.

One day as they were studying with the tutor, who was a priest named Stephen, he gave to them a book of fables, and each read a fable.

Ladislaus read the fable of the

SKY-LARK.

The sky-lark sat on the topmost bough of the savy-tree, and was waked by the first ray of the sun. Then the sky-lark flew and flew up and up to the topmost arch of the sky, and sang the hymn of the morning.

But a frog, who was croaking in the cranberry marsh, said, "Why do you take such pains and fly so high? the sun shines here, and I can sing here."

And the bird said, "God has made me to fly. God has made me to see. I will fly as high as He will lift me, and sing so loud that all shall hear me."

And when the little Prince Ladislaus had read the fable, he cried out, "The sky-lark is the bird for me, and I will paint his picture on my shield after school this morning."

Then the Prince Bela read the next fable,—the fable of the

WATER-RAT.

A good beaver found one day a little water-rat almost dead. His father and mother had been swept away by a freshet, and the little rat was almost starved. But the kind beaver gave him of her own milk, and brought him up in her own lodge with her children, and he got well, and could eat, and swim, and dive with the best of them.

But one day there was a great alarm, that the beavers' dam was giving way before the water. "Come one, come all," said the grandfather of the beavers, "come to the rescue." So they all started, carrying sticks and bark with them, the water-rat and all. But as they swam under an old oak-tree's root, the water-rat stopped in the darkness, and then he quietly turned round and went back to the hut. "It will be hard work," said he "and there are enough of them." There were enough of them. They mended the dam by working all night and by working all day. But, as they came back, a great wave of the freshet came pouring over the dam and, though the dam stood firm, the beavers were swept away,—away and away, down the river into the sea, and they died there.

And the water-rat lived in their grand house by himself, and had all their stores of black-birch bark and willow bark and sweet poplar bark for his own.

"That was a clever rat," said the Prince Bela. "I will paint the rat on my shield, when school is done." And the priest Stephen was very sad when he said so; and the Prince Ladislaus was surprised.

So they went to the play-room and painted their shields. The shields were made of the bark of hemlock-trees. Ladislaus chipped off the rough bark till the shield was white, and made on the place the best sky-lark he could paint there. And Bela watched him, and chipped off the rough bark from his shield, and said, "You paint so well, now paint my water-rat for me." "No," said Ladislaus, though he was very good-natured, "I cannot paint it well. You must paint it yourself." And Bela did so.

II.

So the boys both grew up, and one became King of Hungary, and one was the King of the Bohemians. And King Ladislaus carried on his banner the picture of a sky-lark; and the ladies of the land embroidered sky-larks for the scarfs and for the pennons of the soldiers, and for the motto of the banner were the Latin words "Propior Deo," which mean "Nearer to God." And King Bela carried the water-rat for his cognizance; and the ladies of his land embroidered water-rats for the soldiers; and his motto was "Enough."

And in these times a holy man from Palestine came through all the world; and he told how the pilgrims to the tomb of Christ were beaten and starved by the Saracens, and how many of them were dying in dungeons. And he begged the princes and the lords and ladies, for the love of God and the love of Christ, that they would come and rescue these poor people, and secure the pilgrims in all coming time. And King Ladislaus said to his people, "We will do the best we can, and serve God as He shows us how!" And the people said, "We will do the best we can, and save the people of Christ from the infidel!" And they all came together to the place of arms; and the King chose a hundred of the bravest and healthiest of the young men, all of whom told the truth, and no one of whom was afraid to die, and they marched with him to the land of Christ; and as they marched they sang, "Propior Deo,"—"Nearer to Thee."

And Peter the Hermit went to Bohemia, and told the story of the cruel Saracens and the sufferings of the pilgrims to King Bela and his people. And the King said, "Is it far away?" And the Hermit said, "Far, far away." And the King said, "Ah, well,—they must get out as they got in. We will take care of Bohemia." So the Hermit went on to Saxony, to tell his story.

And King Ladislaus and his hundred true young men rode and rode day by day, and came to the Mount of Olives just in time to be at the side of the great King Godfrey, when he broke the Paynim's walls, and dashed into the city of Jerusalem. And King Ladislaus and his men rode together along the Way of Tears, where Christ bore the cross-beam upon his shoulder, and he sat on the stone where the cross had been reared, and he read the gospel through again; and there he prayed his God that he might always bear his cross bravely, and that, like the Lord Jesus, he might never be afraid to die.

III.

AND when they had all come home to Hungary, their time hung very heavy on their hands. And the young men said to the King, "Lead us to war against the Finns, or lead us to war against the Russ."

But the King said, "No! if they spare our people, we spare their people. Let us have peace." And he called the young men who had fought with him, and he said, "The time hangs heavy with us; let us build a temple here to the living God, and to the honor of his Son. We will carve on its walls the story we have seen, and while we build we will remember Zion and the Way of Tears."

And the young men said, "We are not used to building."

"Nor am I," said the King; "but let us build, and build as best we can, and give to God the best we have and the best we know."

So they dug the deep trenches for the foundations, and they sent north and south, and east and west for the wisest builders who loved the Lord Christ; and the builders came, and the carvers came, and the young men learned to use the chisel and the hammer; and the great Cathedral grew year by year, as a pine-tree in the forest grows above the birches and the yew-trees on the ground.

And once King Bela came to visit his kinsman, and they rode out to see the builders. And King Ladislaus dismounted from his horse, and asked Bela to dismount, and gave to him a chisel and a hammer.

"No," said the King Bela, "it will hurt my hands. In my land we have workmen whom we pay to do these things. But I like to see you work."

So he sat upon his horse till dinner-time, and he went home.

And year by year the Cathedral grew. And a thousand pinnacles were built upon the towers and on the roof and along the walls; and on each pinnacle there fluttered a golden sky-lark. And on the altar in the Cathedral was a scroll of crimson, and on the crimson scroll were letters of gold, and the letters were in the Latin language, and said "Propior Deo," and on a blue scroll underneath, in the language of the people they were translated, and it said, "Nearer to Thee."

IV.

AND another Hermit came, and he told the King that the Black Death was ravaging the cities of the East; that half the people of Constantinople were dead; that the great fair at Adrianople was closed; that the ships on the Black Sea had no sailors; and that there would be no food for the people on the lower river.

And the King said, "Is the Duke dead, whom we saw at Bucharest; is the Emperor dead, who met me at Constantinople?"

"No, your Grace," said the Hermit, "it pleases the Lord that in the Black Death only those die who live in hovels and in towns. The Lord has spared those who live in castles and in palaces."

"Then," said King Ladislaus, "I will live as my people live, and I will die as my people die. The Lord Jesus had no pillow for his head, and no house for his lodging; and as the least of his brethren fares so will I fare, and as I fare so shall they."

So the King and the hundred braves pitched their tents on the high land above the old town, around the new Cathedral, and the Queen and the ladies of the court went with them. And day by day the King and the Queen and the hundred braves and their hundred ladies went up and down the filthy wynds and courts of the city, and they said to the poor people there, "Come, live as we live, and die as we die."

And the people left the holes of pestilence and came and lived in the open air of God.

And when the people saw that the King fared as they fared, the people said, "We also will seek God as the King seeks Him, and will serve Him as he serves Him."

And day by day they found others who had no homes fit for Christian men, and brought them upon the high land and built all together their tents and booths and tabernacles, open to the sun and light, and to the smile and kiss and blessing of the fresh air of God. And there grew a new and beautiful city there.

And so it was, that when the Black Death passed from the East to the West, the Angel of Death left the city of Buda on one side, and the people never saw the pestilence with their eyes. The Angel of Death passed by them, and rested upon the cities of Bohemia.

V.

AND King Ladislaus grew old. His helmet seemed to him more heavy. His sleep seemed to him more coy. But he had little care, for he had a loving wife, and he had healthy, noble sons and daughters, who loved God, and who told the truth, and who were not afraid to die.

But one day, in his happy prosperity, there came to him a messenger running, who said in the Council, "Your Grace, the Red Russians have crossed the Red River of the north, and they are marching with their wives and their children with their men of arms in front, and their wagons behind, and they say they will find a land nearer the sun, and to this land are they coming."

And the old King smiled; and he said to those that were left of the hundred brave men who took the cross with him, "Now we will see if our boys could have fought at Godfrey's side. For us it matters little. One way or another way we shall come nearer to God."

And the armorers mended the old armor, and the young men girded on swords which had never been tried in fight, and the pennons that they bore were embroidered by their sweethearts and sisters as in the old days of the Crusades, and with the same device of a sky-lark in mid-heaven, and the motto, "Nearer, my God, to Thee."

And there came from the great Cathedral the wise men who had come from all the lands. They found the King, and they said to him, "Your Grace, we know how to build the new defences for the land, and we will guard the river ways, that the barbarians shall never enter them."

And when the people knew that the Red Russians were on the way, they met in the square and marched to the palace, and Robert the Smith mounted the steps of the palace and called the King. And he said, "The people are here to bid the King be of good heart. The people bid me say that they will die for their King and for his land."

And the King took from his wife's neck the blue ribbon that she wore, with a golden sky-lark on it, and bound it round the blacksmith's arm, and he said, "If I die, it is nothing; if I live, it is nothing; that is in God's hand. But whether we live or die, let us draw as near Him as we may."

And the Blacksmith Robert turned to the people, and with his loud voice, told what the King had said.

And the people answered in the shout which the Hungarians shout to this day, "Let us die for our king! Let us die for our king!"

And the King called the Queen hastily, and they and their children led the host to the great Cathedral.

And the old priest Stephen, who was ninety years old, stood at the altar, and he read the gospel where it says, "Fear not, little flock, it is your Father's good pleasure to give you the kingdom."

And he read the other gospel where the Lord says, "And I, if I be lifted up, will draw all men unto me." And he read the epistle where it says, "No man liveth to himself, and no man dieth to himself." And he chanted the psalm, "The Lord is my rock, my fortress, and my deliverer."

And fifty thousand men, with one heart and one voice, joined with him. And the King joined, and the Queen to sing, "The Lord is my rock, my fortress, and my deliverer."

And they marched from the Cathedral, singing in the language of the country, "Propior Deo," which is to say in our tongue, "Nearer, my God, to Thee."

And the aged braves who had fought with Godfrey, and the younger men who had learned of arms in the University, went among the people and divided them into companies for the war. And Robert the Blacksmith, and all the guild of the blacksmiths, and of the braziers, and of the coppersmiths, and of the whitesmiths, even the goldsmiths, and the silversmiths, made weapons for the war; and the masons and the carpenters, and the ditchers and delvers marched out with the cathedral builders to the narrow passes of the river, and built new the fortresses.

And the Lady Constance and her daughters, and every lady in the land, went to the churches and the convents, and threw them wide open. And in the kitchens they baked bread for the soldiers; and in the churches they spread couches for the sick or for the wounded.

And when the Red Russians came in their host, there was not a man, or woman, or child in all Hungary but was in the place to which God had called him, and was doing his best in his place for his God, for the Church of Christ, and for his brothers and sisters of the land.

And the host of the Red Russians was turned aside, as at the street corner you have seen the dirty water of a gutter turned aside by the curbstone. They fought one battle against the Hungarian host, and were driven as the blackbirds are driven by the falcons. And they gathered themselves and swept westward; and came down upon the passes to Bohemia.

And there were no fortresses at the entrance to Bohemia; for King Bela had no learned men who loved him. And there was no army in the plains of Bohemia; for his people had been swept away in the pestilence. And there were no brave men who had fought with Godfrey, and knew the art of arms, for in those old days the King had said, "It is far away; and we have 'enough' in Bohemia."

So the Red Russians, who call themselves the Szechs, took his land from him; and they live there till this day. And the King, without a battle, fled from the back-door of his palace, in the disguise of a charcoal-man; and he left his queen and his daughters to be cinder-girls in the service of the Chief of the Red Russians.

And the false charcoal-man walked by day, and walked by night, till he found refuge in the castle of the King Ladislaus; and he met him in the old school-room where they read the fables together. And he remembered how the water-rat came to the home of the beavers.

And he said to King Ladislaus,—

"Ah, me! do you remember when we were boys together? Do you remember the fable of the Sky-lark, and the fable of the Water-rat?"

"I remember both," said the King. And he was silent.

"God has been very kind to you," said the beggar; "and He has been very hard to me."

And the King said nothing.

But the old priest Stephen, said,—

"God is always kind. But God will not give us other fruit than we sow seed for. The King here has tried to serve God as he knew how; with one single eye he has looked on the world of God, and he has made the best choice he knew. And God has given him what he thought not of: brave men for his knights; wise men for his council; a free and loving people for his army. And you have not looked with a single eye; your eye was darkened. You saw only what served yourself. And you said, 'This is enough;' and you had no brave men for your knights; no wise men for your council; no people for your army. You chose to look down, and to take a selfish brute for your adviser. And he has led you so far. We choose to look up; to draw nearer God; and where He leads we follow."

Then King Ladislaus ordered that in the old school-room a bed should be spread for Bela; and that every day his breakfast and his dinner and his supper should be served to him; and he lived there till he died.

THE STORY OF OELLO.

ONCE upon a time there was a young girl, who had the pretty name of Oello. I say, once upon a time, because I do not know when the time was,—nor do I know what the place was,—though my story, in the main, is a true story. I do not mean that I sat by and saw Oello when she wove and when she spun. But I know she did weave and did spin. I do not mean that I heard her speak the word I tell of; for it was many, many hundred years ago. But I do know that she must have said some such words; for I know many of the things which she did, and much of what kind of girl she was.

She grew up like other girls in her country. She did not know how to read. None of them knew how to read. But she knew how to braid straw, and to make fish-nets and to catch fish. She did not know how to spell. Indeed, in that country they had no letters. But she knew how to split open the fish she had caught, how to clean them, how to broil them on the coals, and how to eat them neatly. She had never studied the "analysis of her language." But she knew how to use it like a lady; that is, prettily, simply, without pretence, and always truly. She could sing her baby brother to sleep. She could tell stories to her sisters all day long. And she and they were not afraid when evening came, or when they were in any trouble, to say a prayer aloud to the good God. So they got along, although they could not analyze their language. She knew no geography. She could count her fingers, and the stars in the Southern Cross. She had never seen Orion, or the stars in the Great Bear, or the Pole-Star.

Oello was very young when she married a young kinsman, with whom she had grown up since they were babies. Nobody knows much about him. But he loved her and she loved him. And when morning came they were not afraid to pray to God together,—and when night came she asked her husband to forgive her if she had troubled him, and he asked her to forgive him,—so that their worries and trials never lasted out the day. And they lived a very happy life, till they were very old and died.

There is a bad gap in the beginning of their history. I do not know how it happened. But the first I knew of them, they had left their old home and were wandering alone on foot toward the South. Sometimes I have thought a great earthquake had wrecked their old happy home. Sometimes I have thought there was some horrid pestilence, or fire. No matter what happened, something happened,—so that Oello and her husband, of a hot, very hot day, were alone under a forest of laurels mixed with palms, with bright flowering orchids on them, looking like a hundred butterflies; ferns, half as high as the church is, tossing over them; nettles as large as trees, and tangled vines, threading through the whole. They were tired, oh, how tired! hungry, oh, how hungry! and hot and foot-sore.

"I wish so we were out of this hole," said he to her, "and yet I am afraid of the people we shall find when we come down to the lake side."

"I do not know," said Oello, "why they should want to hurt us."

"I do not know why they should want to," said he, "but I am afraid they will hurt us."

"But we do not want to hurt them," said she. "For my part, all I want is a shelter to live under; and I will help them take care of their children, and

       'I will spin their flax,
           And weave their thread,
      And pound their corn,
           And bake their bread.'"

"How will you tell them that you will do this?" said he.

"I will do it," said Oello, "and that will be better than telling them."

"But do not you just wish," said he, "that you could speak five little words of their language, to say to them that we come as friends, and not as enemies?"

Oello laughed very heartily. "Enemies," said she, "terrible enemies, who have two sticks for their weapons, two old bags for their stores, and cotton clothes for their armor. I do not believe more than half the army will turn out against us." So Oello pulled out the potatoes from the ashes, and found they were baked; she took a little salt from her haversack or scrip, and told her husband that dinner would be ready, if he would only bring some water. He pretended to groan, but went, and came in a few minutes with two gourds full, and they made a very merry meal.

The same evening they came cautiously down on the beautiful meadow land which surrounded the lake they had seen. It is one of the most beautiful countries in the world. It was an hour before sunset,—the hour, I suppose, when all countries are most beautiful. Oello and her husband came joyfully down the hill, through a little track the llamas had made toward the water, wondering at the growth of the wild grasses, and, indeed, the freshness of all the green; when they were startled by meeting a horde of the poor, naked, half-starved Indians, who were just as much alarmed to meet with them.

I do not think that the most stupid of them could have supposed Oello an enemy, nor her husband. For they stepped cheerfully down the path, waving boughs of fresh cinchona as tokens of peace, and looking kindly and pleasantly on the poor Indians, as I believe nobody had looked on them before. There were fifty of the savages, but it was true that they were as much afraid of the two young Northerners as if they had been an army. They saw them coming down the hill, with the western sun behind them, and one of the women cried out, "They are children of the sun, they are children of the sun!" and Oello and her husband looked so as if they had come from a better world that all the other savages believed it.

But the two young people came down so kindly and quickly, that the Indian women could not well run away. And when Oello caught one of the little babies up, and tossed it in her arms, and fondled it, and made it laugh, the little girl's mother laughed too. And when they had all once laughed together, peace was made among them all, and Oello saw where the Indian women had been lying, and what their poor little shelters were, and she led the way there, and sat down on a log that had fallen there, and called the children round her, and began teaching them a funny game with a bit of crimson cord. Nothing pleases savage people or tame people more than attention to their children, and in less time than I have been telling this they were all good friends. The Indian women produced supper. Pretty poor supper it was. Some fresh-water clams from the lake, some snails which Oello really shuddered at, but some bananas which were very nice, and some ulloco, a root Oello had never seen before, and which she thought sickish. But she acted on her motto. "I will do the best I can," she had said all along; so she ate and drank, as if she had always been used to raw snails and to ulloco, and made the wild women laugh by trying to imitate the names of the strange food. In a few minutes after supper the sun set. There is no twilight in that country. When the sun goes down,

> "Like battle target red,—
> He rushes to his burning bed,
> Dyes the whole wave with ruddy light,
> Then sinks at once, and all is night."

The savage people showed the strangers a poor little booth to sleep in, and went away to their own lairs, with many prostrations, for they really thought them "children of the sun."

Oello and her husband laughed very heartily when they knew they were alone. Oello made him promise to go in the morning early for potatoes, and oca, and mashua, which are two other tubers like potatoes which grow there. "And we will show them," said she, "how to cook them." For they had seen by the evening feast, that the poor savage people had no knowledge of the use of fire. So, early in the morning, he went up a little way on the lake shore, and returned with strings of all these roots, and with another string of fish he had caught in a brook above. And when the savage people waked and came to Oello's hut, they found her and her husband just starting their fire,—a feat these people had never seen before.

He had cut with his copper knife a little groove in some soft palm-wood, and he had fitted in it a round piece of iron-wood, and round the iron-wood had bound a bow-string, and while Oello held the palm-wood firm, he made the iron-wood fly round and round and round, till the pith of the palm smoked, and smoked, and at last a flake of the pith caught fire, and then another and another, and Oello dropped other flakes upon these, and blew them gently, and fed them with dry leaves, till they were all in a blaze.

The savage people looked on with wonder and terror. They cried out when they saw the blaze, "They are children of the sun,—they are children of the sun!"—and ran away. Oello and her husband did not know what they said, and went on broiling the fish and baking the potatoes, and the mashua, and the oca, and the ulloco.

And when they were ready, Oello coaxed some of the children to come back, and next their mothers came and next the men. But still they said,

"They are children of the sun." And when they ate of the food that had been cooked for them, they said it was the food of the immortals.

Now, in Oello's home, this work of making the fire from wood had been called menial work, and was left to servants only. But even the princes of that land were taught never to order another to do what they could not do themselves. And thus it happened that the two young travellers could do it so well. And thus it was, that, because they did what they could, the savage people honored them with such exceeding honor, and because they did the work of servants they called them gods. As it is written: "He who is greatest among you shall be your servant."

And this was much the story of that day and many days. While her husband went off with the men, taught them how he caught the fish, and how they could catch huanacos, Oello sat in the shade with the children, who were never tired of pulling at the crimson cord around her waist, and at the tassels of her head-dress. All savage children are curious about the dress of their visitors. So it was easy for Oello to persuade them to go with her and pick tufts of wild cotton, till they had quite a store of it, and then to teach them to spin it on distaffs she made for them from laurel-wood, and at last to braid it and to knit it,—till at last one night, when the men came home, Oello led out thirty of the children in quite a grand procession, dressed all of them in pretty cotton suits they had knit for themselves, instead of the filthy, greasy skins they had always worn before. This was a great triumph for Oello; but when the people would gladly have worshipped her, she only said, "I did what I could,—I did what I could,—say no more, say no more."

And as the year passed by, she and her husband taught the poor people how, if they would only plant the maize, they could have all they wanted in the winter, and if they planted the roots of the ulloco, and the oca, and the mashua, and the potato, they would have all they needed of them; how they might make long fish-ways for the fish, and pitfalls for the llama. And they learned the language of the poor people, and taught them the language to which they themselves were born. And year by year their homes grew neater and more cheerful. And year by year the children were stronger and better. And year by year the world in that part of it was more and more subdued to the will and purpose of a good God. And whenever Manco,

Oello's husband, was discouraged, she always said, "We will do the best we can," and always it proved that that was all that a good God wanted them to do.

It was from the truth and steadiness of those two people, Manco and Oello, that the great nation of Peru was raised up from a horde of savages, starving in the mountains, to one of the most civilized and happy nations of their times. Unfortunately for their descendants, they did not learn the use of iron or gunpowder, so that the cruel Spaniards swept them and theirs away. But for hundreds of years they lived peacefully and happily,— growing more and more civilized with every year, because the young Oello and her husband Manco had done what they could for them.

They did not know much. But what they knew they could do. They were not, so far as we know, skilful in talking. But they were cheerful in acting.

They did not hide their light under a bushel. They made it shine on all that came around. Their duties were the humblest, only making a fire in the morning, cleaning potatoes and cooking them, spinning, braiding, twisting, and weaving. This was the best Oello could do. She did that, and in doing it she reared an empire. We can contrast her life with that of the savages around her. As we can see a drop of blood when it falls into a cup of water, we can see how that one life swayed theirs. If she had lived among her kindred, and done at home these simple things, we should never have heard her name. But none the less would she have done them. None the less, year in and year out, century in and century out, would that sweet, loving, true, unselfish life have told in God's service. And he would have known it, though you and I—who are we?—had never heard her name!

Forgotten! do not ever think that anything is forgotten!

LOVE IS THE WHOLE.

A STORY FOR CHILDREN.

THIS is a story about some children who were living together in a Western State, in a little house on the prairie, nearly two miles from any other. There were three boys and three girls; the oldest girl was seventeen, and her oldest brother a year younger. Their mother had died two or three years before, and now their father grew sick,—more sick and more, and died also. The children were taking the best care they could of him, wondering and watching. But no care could do much, and so he told them. He told them all that he should not live long; but that when he died he should not be far from them, and should be with their dear mother. "Remember," he said, "to love each other. Be kind to each other. Stick together, if you can. Or, if you separate, love one another as if you were together." He did not say any more then. He lay still awhile, with his eyes closed; but every now and then a sweet smile swept over his face, so that they knew he was awake. Then he roused up once more, and said, "Love is the whole, George; love is the whole,"—and so he died.

I have no idea that the children, in the midst of their grief and loneliness, took in his meaning. But afterwards they remembered it again and again, and found out why he said it to them.

Any of you would have thought it a queer little house. It was not a log cabin. They had not many logs there. But it was no larger than the log cabin which General Grant is building in the picture. There was a little entry-way at one end, and two rooms opening on the right as you went. A flight of steps went up into the loft, and in the loft the boys slept in two beds. This was all. But if they had no rooms for servants, on the other hand they had no servants for rooms. If they had no hot-water pipes, on the other hand a large kettle hung on the crane above the kitchen fire, and there was but a very short period of any day that one could not dip out hot water. They had no gas-pipes laid through the house. But they went to bed the earlier, and were the more sure to enjoy the luxury of the great morning illumination by the sun. They lost but few steps in going from room to room. They were never troubled for want of fresh air. They had no door-bell, so no guest was ever left waiting in the cold. And though they had no speaking-tubes in the house, still they found no difficulty in calling each other if Ethan were up stairs and Alice wanted him to come down.

Their father was buried, and the children were left alone. The first night after the funeral they stole to their beds as soon as they could, after the mock supper was over. The next morning George and Fanny found themselves the first to meet at the kitchen hearth. Each had tried to anticipate the other in making the morning fire. Each confessed to the other that there had been but little sleep, and that the night had seemed hopelessly long.

"But I have thought it all over," said the brave, stout boy. "Father told us to stick together as long as we can. And I know I can manage it. The children will all do their best when they understand it. And I know, though father could not believe it, I know that I can manage with the team. We will never get in debt. I shall never drink. Drink and debt, as he used to say, are the only two devils. Never you cry, darling Fanny, I know we can get along."

"George," said Fanny, "I know we can get along if you say so. I know it will be very hard upon you. There are so many things the other young men do which you will not be able to do; and so many things which they have which you might have. But none of them has a sister who loves them as I love you. And, as he said, 'Love is the whole.'"

I suppose those words over the hearth were almost the only words of sentiment which ever passed between those two about their plans. But from that moment those plans went forward more perfectly than if they had been talked over at every turn, and amended every day. That is the way with all true stories of hearth and home.

For instance, it was only that evening, when the day's work of all the six was done—and for boys and girls, it was hard work, too—Fanny and George would have been glad enough, both of them, to take each a book, and have the comfort of resting and reading. But George saw that the younger girls looked down-cast and heavy, and that the boys were whispering round the door-steps as if they wanted to go down to the blacksmith's shop by way of getting away from the sadness of the house. He hated to have them begin the habit of loafing there, with all the lazy boys and men from three miles round. And so he laid down his book, and said, as cheerily as if he had not laid his father's body in the grave the day before,—

"What shall we do to-night that we can all do together? Let us have something that we have never had before. Let us try what Mrs. Chisholm told us about. Let us act a ballad."

Of course the children were delighted with acting. George knew that, and Fanny looked across so gratefully to him, and laid her book away also; and, in a minute, Ethan, the young carpenter of the family, was putting up sconces for tallow candles to light the scenes, and Fanny had Sarah and Alice out in the wood-house, with the shawls, and the old ribbons, and strips of bright calico, which made up the dresses, and George instructed Walter as to the way in which he should arrange his armor and his horse, and so, after a period of preparation, which was much longer than the period of performance, they got ready to act in the kitchen the ballad of Lochinvar.

The children had a happy evening. They were frightened when they went to bed—the little ones—because they had been so merry. They came together with George and Fanny, and read their Bible as they had been used to do with their father, and the last text they read was, "Love is the fulfilling of the law." So the little ones went to bed, and left George and Fanny again together.

"Pretty hard, was it not?" said she, smiling through her tears. "But it is so much best for them that home should be the happiest place of all for them. After all, 'Love is the whole.'"

And that night's sacrifice, which the two older children made to the younger brothers and sisters as it were over their father's grave, was the beginning of many such nights, and of many other joint amusements which the children arranged together. They read Dickens aloud. They cleared out the corn-room at the end of the wood-house for a place for their dialogues and charades. The neighbors' children liked to come in, and, under very strict rules of early hours and of good behavior, they came. And George and Fanny found, not only that they were getting a reputation for keeping their own little flock in order, but that the nicest children all around were intrusted to their oversight, even by the most careful fathers and mothers. All this pleasure to the children came from the remembrance that "Love is the whole."

Far from finding themselves a lonely and forsaken family, these boys and girls soon found that they were surrounded with friends. George was quite right in assuming that he could manage the team, and could keep the little farm up, not to its full production under his father, but to a crop large enough to make them comfortable. Every little while there had to be a consultation. Mr. Snyder came down one day to offer him forty dollars a month and his board, if he would go off on a surveying party and carry chain for the engineers. It would be in a good line for promotion. Forty dollars a month to send home to Fanny was a great temptation. And George and Fanny put an extra pine-knot on the fire, after the children had gone to bed, that they might talk it over. But George declined the proposal, with many thanks to Mr. Snyder. He said to him, "that, if he went away, the whole household would be very much weakened. The boys could not carry on the farm alone, and would have to hire out. He thought they were too young for that. After all, Mr. Snyder, 'Love is the whole.'" And Mr. Snyder agreed with him.

Then, as a few years passed by, after another long council, in which another pine-knot was sacrificed on the hearth, and in which Walter assisted with George and Fanny, it was agreed that Walter should "hire out." He had "a chance," as they said, to go over to the Stacy Brothers, in the next county. Now the Stacy Brothers had the greatest stock farm in all that part of Illinois. They had to hire a great deal of help, and it was a great question to George and Fanny whether poor Walter might not get more harm than good there. But they told Walter perfectly frankly their doubts and their hopes. And he said boldly, "Never you fear me. Do you think I am such a fool as to forget? Do I not know that 'Love is the whole'? Shall I ever forget who taught us so?" And so it was determined that he should go.

Yes, and he went. The Stacys' great establishment was different indeed from the little cabin he had left. But the other boys there, and the men he met, Norwegians, Welshmen, Germans, Yankees, all sorts of people, all had hearts just like his heart. And a helpful boy, honest as a clock and brave as St. Paul, who really tried to serve every one as he found opportunity, made friends on the great stock farm just as he had in the corn-room at the end of the wood-house. And once a month, when their wages were paid, he was able to send home the lion's share of his to Fanny, in letters which every month were written a little better, and seemed a little more easy for him to write. And when Thanksgiving came, Mr. George Stacy sent him home for a fortnight, with a special message to his sister, "that he could not do without him, and he wished she would send him a dozen of such boys. He knew how to raise oxen, he said; but would Miss Fanny tell him how she brought up boys like Walter?"

"I could have told him," said Walter, "but I did not choose to; I could have told him that love was the whole."

And that story of Walter is only the story of the way in which Ethan also kept up the home tie, and came back, when he got a chance, from his voyages. His voyages were not on the sea. He "hired out" with a canal-boatman. Sometimes they went to the lake, and once they set sail there and came as far as Cleveland. Ethan made a great deal of fun in pretending to tell great sea-stories, like Swiss Family Robinson and Sinbad the Sailor. Fresh-water voyaging has its funny side, as has the deep-sea sailing. But Ethan did not hold to it long. His experience with grain brought him at last to Chicago, and he engaged there in the work of an elevator. But he lived always the old home life. There were three other boys he got acquainted with, one at Mr. Eggleston's church, one at the Custom House, and one at the place where he got his dinner, and they used to come up to his little room in the seventh story of the McKenzie House, and sit on his bed and in his chairs, just as the boys from the blacksmith's came into the corn-room. These four boys made a literary club "for reading Shakespeare and the British essayists." Often did they laugh afterwards at its title. They called it the Club of the Tetrarchy, because they thought it grand to have a Greek name. Whatever its name was, it kept them out of mischief. These boys grew up to be four ruling powers in Western life. And when, years after, some one asked Ethan how it was that he had so stanch a friend in Torrey, Ethan told the history of the seventh-story room at the McKenzie House, and he said, "Love is the whole."

Central in all his life was the little cabin of two rooms and a loft over it. There is no day of his life, from that time to this, of which Fanny cannot tell you the story from his weekly letters home. For though she does not live in the cabin now, she keeps the old letters filed and in order, and once a week steadily Ethan has written to her, and the letters are all sealed now with his own seal-ring, and on the seal-ring is carved the inscription, "Love is the whole."

I must not try to tell you the story of Alice's fortunes, or Sarah's. Every day of their lives was a romance, as is every day of yours and mine. Every day was a love-story, as may be every day of yours and mine, if we will make it so. As they all grew older their homes were all somewhat parted. The boys became men and married. The girls became women and married. George never pulled down the old farm-house, not even when he and Mr. Vaux built the beautiful house that stands next to it to-day. He put trellises on the sides of it. He trained cotoneaster and Roxbury wax-work over it. He carved a cross himself, and fastened it in the gable. Above the door, as you went in, was a picture of Mary Mother and her Child, with this inscription:
—

> "Holy cell and holy shrine,
>   For the Maid and Child divine!
> Remember, thou that seest her bending
>   O'er that babe upon her knee,
> All heaven is ever thus extending
>   Its arms of love round thee.
> Such love shall bless our archèd porch;
> Crowned with his cross, our cot becomes a church."

And in that little church he gathered the boys and girls of the neighborhood every Sunday afternoon, and told them stories and they sang together. And on the week days he got up children's parties there, which all the children thought rather the best experiences of the week, and he and his wife and his own children grew to think the hours in the cabin the best hours of all. There were pictures on the walls; they painted the windows themselves with flower-pictures, and illuminated them with colored leaves. But there were but two inscriptions. These were over the inside of the two doors, and both inscriptions were the same,—"Love is the whole."

They told all these stories, and a hundred more, at a great Thanksgiving party after the war. Walter and his wife and his children came from Sangamon County; and the General and all his family came down from Winetka; and Fanny and the Governor and all their seven came all the way from Minnesota; and Alice and her husband and all her little ones came up the river, and so across from Quincy; and Sarah and Gilbert, with the twins and the babies, came in their own carriage all the way from Horace. So there was a Thanksgiving dinner set for all the six, and the six husbands and wives, and the twenty-seven children. In twenty years, since their father died, those brothers and sisters had lived for each other. They had had separate houses, but they had spent the money in them for each other. No one of them had said that anything he had was his own. They had confided wholly each in each. They had passed through much sorrow, and in that sorrow had strengthened each other. They had passed through much joy, and the joy had been multiplied tenfold because it was joy that was shared. At the Thanksgiving they acted the ballad of Lochinvar again, or rather some of the children did. And that set Fanny the oldest and Sarah the youngest to telling to the oldest nephews and nieces some of the stories of the cabin days. But Fanny said, when the children asked for more, "There is no need of any more,—'Love is the whole.'"

CHRISTMAS AND ROME.

THE first Christmas this in which a Roman Senate has sat in Rome since the old-fashioned Roman Senates went under,—or since they "went up," if we take the expressive language of our Chicago friends.

And Pius IX. is celebrating Christmas with an uncomfortable look backward, and an uncomfortable look forward, and an uncomfortable look all around. It is a suggestive matter, this Italian Parliament sitting in Rome. It suggests a good deal of history and a good deal of prophecy.

"They say" (whoever they may be) that somewhere in Rome there is a range of portraits of popes, running down from never so far back; that only one niche was left in the architecture, which received the portrait of Pius IX., and that then that place was full. Maybe it is so. I did not see the row. But I have heard the story a thousand times. Be it true, be it false, there are, doubtless, many other places where portraits of coming popes could be hung. There is a little wall-room left in the City Hall of New York. There are, also, other palaces in which popes could live. Palaces are as plenty in America as are Pullman cars. But it is possible that there are no such palaces in Rome.

So this particular Christmas sets one careering back a little, to look at that mysterious connection of Rome with Christianity, which has held on so steadily since the first Christmas got itself put on historical record by a Roman census-maker. Humanly speaking, it was nothing more nor less than a Roman census which makes the word Bethlehem to be a sacred word over all the world to-day. To any person who sees the humorous contrasts of history there is reason for a bit of a smile when he thinks of the way this census came into being, and then remembers what came of it. Here was a consummate movement of Augustus, who would fain have the statistics of his empire. Such excellent things are statistics! "You can prove anything by statistics," says Mr. Canning, "except—the truth." So Augustus orders his census, and his census is taken. This Quirinus, or Quirinius, pro-consul of Syria, was the first man who took it there, says the Bible. Much appointing of marshals and deputy-marshals,—men good at counting, and good at writing, and good at collecting fees! Doubtless it was a great staff achievement of Quirinus, and made much talk in its time. And it is so well condensed at last and put into tables with indexes and averages as to be very creditable, I will not doubt, to the census bureau. But alas! as time rolls on, things change, so that this very Quirinus, who with all a pro-consul's power took such pains to record for us the number of people there were in Bethlehem and in Judah, would have been clean forgotten himself, and his census too, but that things turned bottom upward. The meanest child born in Bethlehem when this census business was going on happened to prove to be King of the World. It happened that he overthrew the dynasty of Cæsar Augustus, and his temples, and his empire. It happened that everything which was then established tottered and fell, as the star of this child arose. And the child's star did rise. And now this Publius Sulpicius Quirinus or Quirinius,—a great man in his day, for whom Augustus asked for a triumph,—is rescued from complete forgetfulness because that baby happened to be born in Syria when his census was going on!

I always liked to think that some day when Augustus Cæsar was on a state visit to the Temple of Fortune some attentive clerk handed him down the roll which had just come in and said, "From Syria, your Highness!" that he might have a chance to say something to the Emperor; that the Emperor thanked him, and, in his courtly way, opened the roll so as to seem interested; that his eye caught the words "Bethlehem—village near Jerusalem," and the figures which showed the number of the people and of the children and of all the infants there. Perhaps. No matter if not. Sixty years after, Augustus' successor, Nero, set fire to Rome in a drunken fit. The Temple of Fortune caught the flames, and our roll, with Bethlehem and the count of Joseph's possessions twisted and crackled like any common rag, turned to smoke and ashes, and was gone. That is what such statistics come to!

Five hundred years after, the whole scene is changed. The Church of Christ, which for hundreds of years worshipped under-ground in Rome, has found air and sunlight now. It is almost five hundred years after Paul enters Rome as a prisoner, after Nero burned Rome down, that a monk of St. Andrew, one of the more prominent monasteries of the city of Rome, walking through that great market-place of the city—which to this hour preserves most distinctly, perhaps, the memory of what Rome was—saw a party of fair-haired slaves for sale among the rest. He stops to ask where they come from, and of what nation they are; to be told they are "Angli." "Rather Angeli," says Gregory,—"rather angels;" and with other sacred *bon-mots* he fixes the pretty boys and pretty girls in his memory. Nor are these familiar plays upon words to be spoken of as mere puns. Gregory was determined to attempt the conversion of the land from which these "angels" came. He started on the pilgrimage, which was then a dangerous one; but was recalled by the pope of his day, at the instance of his friends, who could not do without him.

A few years more and this monk is Bishop of Rome. True to the promise of the market-place, he organizes the Christian mission which fulfils his prophecy. He sends Austin with his companions to the island of the fair-haired slave boys; and that new step in the civilization of that land comes, to which we owe it that we are met in this church, nay, that we live in this land this day.

So far has the star of the baby of Bethlehem risen in a little more than five centuries. A Christian dominion has laid its foundations in the Eternal City. And you and I, gentle reader, are what we are and are where we are because that monk of St. Andrew saw those angel boys that day in a Roman market-place.

THE SURVIVOR'S STORY.

FORTUNATELY we were with our wives.

It is in general an excellent custom, as I will explain if opportunity is given.

First, you are thus sure of good company.

For four mortal hours we had ground along, and stopped and waited and started again, in the drifts between Westfield and Springfield. We had shrieked out our woes by the voices of fire-engines. Brave men had dug. Patient men had sate inside, and waited for the results of the digging. At last, in triumph, at eleven and three-quarters, as they say in Cinderella, we entered the Springfield station.

It was Christmas eve!

Leaving the train to its devices, Blatchford and his wife (her name was Sarah), and I with mine (her name was Phebe), walked quickly with our little sacks out of the station, ploughed and waded along the white street, not to the Massasoit,—no, but to the old Eagle and Star, which was still standing, and was a favorite with us youngsters. Good waffles, maple syrup *ad lib.*, such fixings of other sorts as we preferred, and some liberty. The amount of liberty in absolutely first-class hotels is but small. A drowsy boy waked, and turned up the gas. Blatchford entered our names on the register, and cried at once, "By George, Wolfgang is here, and Dick! What luck!" for Dick and Wolfgang also travel with their wives. The boy explained that they had come up the river in the New-Haven train, were only nine hours behind time, had arrived at ten, and had just finished supper and gone to bed. We ordered rare beef-steak, waffles, dip-toast, omelettes with kidneys, and omelettes without; we toasted our feet at the open fire in the parlor; we ate the supper when it was ready; and we also went to bed; rejoicing that we had home with us, having travelled with our wives; and that we could keep our merry Christmas here. If only Wolfgang and Dick and their wives would join us, all would be well. (Wolfgang's wife was named Bertha, and Dick's was named Hosanna,—a name I have never met with elsewhere.)

Bed followed; and I am a graceless dog that I do not write a sonnet here on the unbroken slumber that followed. Breakfast, by arrangement of us four, at nine. At 9.30, to us enter Bertha, Dick, Hosanna, and Wolfgang, to name them in alphabetical order. Four chairs had been turned down for them. Four chops, four omelettes, and four small oval dishes of fried potatoes had been ordered, and now appeared. Immense shouting, immense kissing among those who had that privilege, general wondering, and great congratulating that our wives were there. Solid resolution that we would advance no farther. Here, and here only, in Springfield itself, would we celebrate our Christmas day.

It may be remarked in parenthesis that we had learned already that no train had entered the town since eleven and a quarter; and it was known by telegraph that none was within thirty-four miles and a half of the spot, at the moment the vow was made.

We waded and ploughed our way through the snow to church. I think Mr. Rumfry, if that is the gentleman's name who preached an admirable Christmas sermon, in a beautiful church there is, will remember the platoon of four men and four women, who made perhaps a fifth of his congregation in that storm, —a storm which shut off most church-going. Home again; a jolly fire in the parlor, dry stockings, and dry slippers. Turkeys, and all things fitting for the dinner; and then a general assembly, not in a caravanserai, not in a coffee-room, but in the regular guests' parlor of a New-England second-class hotel, where, as it was ordered, there were no "transients" but ourselves that day; and whence all the "boarders" had gone either to their own rooms, or to other homes.

For people who have their wives with them, it is not difficult to provide entertainment on such an occasion.

"Bertha," said Wolfgang, "could you not entertain us with one of your native dances?"

"Ho! slave," said Dick to Hosanna, "play upon the virginals." And Hosanna played a lively Arab air on the tavern piano, while the fair Bertha danced with a spirit unusual. Was it indeed in memory of the Christmas of her own dear home in Circassia?

All that, from "Bertha" to "Circassia," is not so. We did not do this at all. That was all a slip of the pen. What we did was this. John Blatchford pulled the bell-cord till it broke (they always break in novels, and sometimes they do in taverns). This bell-cord broke. The sleepy boy came; and John said, "Caitiff, is there never a barber in the house?" The frightened boy said there was; and John bade him send him. In a minute the barber appeared,—black, as was expected,—with a shining face, and white teeth, and in shirt sleeves, and broad grins. "Do you tell me, Cæsar," said John, "that in your country they do not wear their coats on Christmas day?"—"Sartin, they do, sir, when they go out doors."

"Do you tell me, Cæsar," said Dick, "that they have doors in your country?"—"Sartin, they do," said poor Cæsar, flurried.

"Boy," said I, "the gentlemen are making fun of you. They want to know if you ever keep Christmas in your country without a dance."

"Never, sar," said poor Cæsar.

"Do they dance without music?"

"No, sar; never."

"Go, then," I said in my sternest accents,—"go fetch a zittern, or a banjo, or a kit, or a hurdy-gurdy, or a fiddle."

The black boy went, and returned with his violin. And as the light grew gray, and crept into the darkness, and as the darkness gathered more thick and more, he played for us and he played for us, tune after tune; and we danced,—first with precision, then in sport, then in wild holiday frenzy. We began with waltzes,—so great is the convenience of travelling with your wives,—where should we have been, had we been all sole alone, four men? Probably playing whist or euchre. And now we began with waltzes, which passed into polkas, which subsided into round dances; and then in very exhaustion we fell back in a grave quadrille. I danced with Hosanna; Wolfgang and Sarah were our *vis-à-vis*. We went through the same set that Noah and his three boys danced in the ark with their four wives, and which has been danced ever since, in every moment, on one or another spot of the dry earth, going round it with the sun, like the drumbeat of England,—right and left, first two forward, right hand across, *pastorale*,—the whole series of them; we did them with as much spirit as if it had been on a flat on the side of Ararat, ground yet too muddy for croquet. Then Blatchford called for "Virginia Reel," and we raced and chased through that. Poor Cæsar began to get exhausted, but a little flip from down stairs helped him amazingly. And, after the flip, Dick cried, "Can you not dance 'Money-Musk'?" And in one wild frenzy of delight we danced "Money-Musk" and "Hull's Victory" and "Dusty Miller" and "Youth's Companion," and "Irish Jigs" on the closet-door lifted off for the occasion, till the men lay on the floor screaming with the fun, and the women fell back on the sofas, fairly faint with laughing.

All this last, since the sentence after "Circassia," is a mistake. There was not any bell, nor any barber, and we did not dance at all. This was all a slip of my memory.

What we really did was this:—

John Blatchford said,—"Let us all tell stories." It was growing dark and he had put more logs on the fire.

Bertha said,—

> "Heap on more wood, the wind is chill;
> But let it whistle as it will,
> We'll keep our merry Christmas still."

She said that because it was in "Bertha's Visit," a very stupid book which she remembered.

Then Wolfgang told

THE PENNY-A-LINER'S STORY.

[Wolfgang is a reporter, or was then, on the staff of the "Star."]

When I was on the "Tribune" (he never was on the "Tribune" an hour, unless he calls selling the "Tribune" at Fort Plains being on the "Tribune"). But I tell the story as he told it. He said,—

When I was on the "Tribune," I was despatched to report Mr. Webster's great reply to Hayne. This was in the days of stages. We had to ride from Baltimore to Washington early in the morning to get there in time. I found my boots were gone from my room when the stage-man called me, and I reported that speech in worsted slippers my wife had given me the week before. As we came into Bladensburg it grew light, and I recognized my boots on the feet of my fellow-passenger,—there was but one other man in the stage. I turned to claim them, but stopped in a moment, for it was Webster himself. How serene his face looked as he slept there! He woke soon, passed the time of day, offered me a part of a sandwich,—for we were old friends,—I was counsel against him in the Ogden case. Said Webster to me,—"Steele, I am bothered about this speech: I have a paragraph in it which I cannot word up to my mind." And he repeated it to me. "How would this do?" said he. "'Let us hope that the sense of unrestricted freedom may be so intertwined with the desire to preserve a connection of the several parts of the body politic, that some arrangement, more or less lasting, may prove in a measure satisfactory.' How would that do?"

I said I liked the idea, but the expression seemed involved.

"And it is involved," said Webster; "but I can't improve it."

"How would this do?" said I.

"'LIBERTY AND UNION, NOW AND FOREVER, ONE AND INSEPARABLE!'"

"Capital!" he said, "capital! write that down for me." At that moment we arrived at the Capitol steps. I wrote down the words for him, and from my notes he read them, when that place in the speech came along.

All of us applauded the story.

Phebe then told

THE SCHOOLMISTRESS'S STORY.

You remind me of the impression that very speech made on me, as I heard Henry Chapin deliver it at an exhibition at Leicester Academy. I resolved then that I would free the slave, or perish in the attempt. But how? I, a woman,—disfranchised by the law? Ha! I saw!

I went to Arkansas. I opened a "Normal College, or Academy for Teachers." We had balls every second night, to make it popular. Immense numbers came. Half the teachers of the Southern States were trained there. I had admirable instructors in Oil Painting and Music,—the most essential studies. The Arithmetic I taught myself. I taught it well. I achieved fame. I achieved wealth; invested in Arkansas Five per Cents. Only one secret device I persevered in. To all,—old and young, innocent girls and sturdy men,—I so taught the multiplication-table, that one fatal error was hidden in its array of facts. The nine line is the difficult one. I buried the error there. "Nine times six," I taught them, "is fifty-six." The rhyme made it easy. The gilded falsehood passed from lip to lip, from State to State,—one little speck in a chain of golden verity. I retired from teaching. Slowly I watched the growth of the rebellion. At last the aloe blossom shot up,—after its hundred years of waiting. The Southern heart was fired. I brooded over my revenge. I repaired to Richmond. I opened a first-class boarding-house, where all the Cabinet, and most of the Senate, came for their meals; and I had eight permanents. Soon their brows clouded. The first flush of victory passed away. Night after night, they sat over their calculations, which all came wrong. I smiled,—and was a villain! None of their sums would prove. None of their estimates matched the performance! Never a muster-roll that fitted as it should do! And I,—the despised boarding-mistress,—I alone knew why! Often and often, when Memminger has said to me, with an oath, "Why this discordancy in our totals?" have my lips burned to tell the secret! But no! I hid it in my bosom. And when, at last, I saw a black regiment march into Richmond, singing "John Brown," I cried, for the first time in twenty years, "Nine times six is fifty-four;" and gloated in my sweet revenge.

Then was hushed the harp of Phebe, and Dick told his story.

THE INSPECTOR OF GAS-METERS' STORY.

Mine is a tale of the ingratitude of republics. It is well-nigh thirty years since I was walking by the Owego and Ithaca Railroad,—a crooked road, not then adapted to high speed. Of a sudden I saw that a long cross timber, on a trestle, high above a swamp, had sprung up from its ties. I looked for a spike with which to secure it. I found a stone with which to hammer the spike. But, at this moment, a train approached, down hill. I screamed. They heard! But the engine had no power to stop the heavy train. With the presence of mind of a poet, and the courage of a hero, I flung my own weight on the fatal timber. I would hold it down, or perish. The engine came. The elasticity of the pine timber whirled me in the air! But I held on. The tender crossed. Again I was flung in wild gyrations. But I held on. "It is no bed of roses," I said; "but what act of Parliament was there that I should be happy." Three passenger cars, and ten freight cars, as was then the vicious custom of that road, passed me. But I held on, repeating to myself texts of Scripture to give me courage. As the last car passed, I was whirled into the air by the rebound of the rafter. "Heavens!" I said, "if my orbit is a hyperbola, I shall never return to earth." Hastily I estimated its ordinates, and calculated the curve. What bliss! It was a parabola! After a flight of a hundred and seventeen cubits, I landed, head down, in a soft mud-hole.

In that train was the young U. S. Grant, on his way to West Point for examination. But for me the armies of the Republic would have had no leader.

I pressed my claim, when I asked to be appointed to England. Although no one else wished to go, I alone was forgotten. Such is gratitude with republics!

He ceased. Then Sarah Blatchford told

THE WHEELER AND WILSON'S OPERATIVE'S STORY.

My father had left the anchorage of Sorrento for a short voyage, if voyage it may be called. Life was young, and this world seemed heaven. The yacht bowled on under close-reefed stay-sails, and all was happy. Suddenly the corsairs seized us: all were slain in my defence; but I,—this fatal gift of beauty bade them spare my life!

Why linger on my tale! In the Zenana of the Shah of Persia I found my home. "How escape his eye?" I said; and, fortunately, I remembered that in my reticule I carried one box of F. Kidder's indelible ink. Instantly I applied the liquid in the large bottle to one cheek. Soon as it was dry, I applied that in the small bottle, and sat in the sun one hour. My head ached with the sunlight, but what of that? I was a fright, and I knew all would be well.

I was consigned, so soon as my hideous deficiencies were known, to the sewing-room. Then how I sighed for my machine! Alas! it was not there; but I constructed an imitation from a cannon-wheel, a coffee-mill, and two nut-crackers. And with this I made the under-clothing for the palace and the Zenana.

I also vowed revenge. Nor did I doubt one instant how; for in my youth I had read Lucretia Borgia's memoirs, and I had a certain rule for slowly slaying a tyrant at a distance. I was in charge of the shah's own linen. Every week, I set back the buttons on his shirt collars by the width of one thread; or, by arts known to me, I shrunk the binding of the collar by a like proportion. Tighter and tighter with each week did the vice close around his larynx. Week by week, at the high religious festivals, I could see his face was blacker and blacker. At length the hated tyrant died. The leeches called it apoplexy. I did not undeceive them. His guards sacked the palace. I bagged the diamonds, fled with them to Trebizond, and sailed thence in a caïque to South Boston. No more! such memories oppress me.

Her voice was hushed. I told my tale in turn.

THE CONDUCTOR'S STORY.

I was poor. Let this be my excuse, or rather my apology. I entered a Third Avenue car at Thirty-sixth Street, and saw the conductor sleeping. Satan tempted me, and I took from him his badge, 213. I see the hated figures now. When he woke, he knew not he had lost it. The car started, and he walked to the rear. With the badge on my coat, I collected eight fares within, stepped forward, and sprang into the street. Poverty is my only apology for the crime. I concealed myself in a cellar where men were playing with props. Fear is my only excuse. Lest they should suspect me, I joined their game, and my forty cents were soon three dollars and seventy. With these ill-gotten gains, I visited the gold exchange, then open evenings. My superior intelligence enabled me to place well my modest means, and at midnight I had a competence. Let me be a warning to all young men. Since that night, I have never gambled more.

I threw the hated badge into the river. I bought a palace on Murray Hill, and led an upright and honorable life. But since that night of terror the sound of the horse-cars oppresses me. Always since, to go up town or down, I order my own coupé, with George to drive me; and never have I entered the cleanly, sweet, and airy carriage provided for the public. I cannot; conscience is too much for me. You see in me a monument of crime.

I said no more. A moment's pause, a few natural tears, and a single sigh hushed the assembly; then Bertha, with her siren voice, told—

THE WIFE OF BIDDEFORD'S STORY.

At the time you speak of, I was the private governess of two lovely boys, Julius and Pompey,—Pompey the senior of the two. The black-eyed darling! I see him now. I also see, hanging to his neck, his blue-eyed brother, who had given Pompey his black eye the day before. Pompey was generous to a fault; Julius, parsimonious beyond virtue. I therefore instructed them in two different rooms. To Pompey, I read the story of "Waste not, want not." To Julius, on the other hand, I spoke of the All-love of his great Mother Nature, and her profuse gifts to her children. Leaving him with grapes and oranges, I stepped back to Pompey, and taught him how to untie parcels so as to save the string. Leaving him winding the string neatly, I went back to Julius, and gave to him ginger-cakes. The dear boys grew from year to year. They outgrew their knickerbockers, and had trousers. They outgrew their jackets, and became men; and I felt that I had not lived in vain. I had conquered nature. Pompey, the little spendthrift, was the honored cashier of a savings bank, till he ran away with the capital. Julius, the miser, became the chief croupier at the New Crockford's. One of those boys is now in Botany Bay, and the other is in Sierra Leone!

"I thought you were going to say in a hotter place," said John Blatchford; and he told his story:—

THE STOKER'S STORY.

We were crossing the Atlantic in a Cunarder. I was second stoker on the starboard watch. In that horrible gale we spoke of before dinner, the coal was exhausted, and I, as the best-dressed man, was sent up to the captain to ask what we should do. I found him himself at the wheel. He almost cursed me and bade me say nothing of coal, at a moment when he must keep her head to the wind with her full power, or we were lost. He bade me slide my hand into his pocket, and take out the key of the after freight-room, open that, and use the contents for fuel. I returned hastily to the engine-room, and we did as we were bid. The room contained nothing but old account books, which made a hot and effective fire.

On the third day the captain came down himself into the engine-room, where I had never seen him before, called me aside, and told me that by mistake he had given me the wrong key; asking me if I had used it. I pointed to him the empty room: not a leaf was left. He turned pale with fright. As I saw his emotion he confided to me the truth. The books were the evidences or accounts of the British national debt; of what is familiarly known as the Consolidated Fund, or the "Consols." They had been secretly sent to New York for the examination of James Fiske, who had been asked to advance a few millions on this security to the English Exchequer, and now all evidence of indebtedness was gone!

The captain was about to leap into the sea. But I dissuaded him. I told him to say nothing; I would keep his secret; no man else knew it. The Government would never utter it. It was safe in our hands. He reconsidered his purpose. We came safe to port and did—nothing.

Only on the first quarter-day which followed, I obtained leave of absence, and visited the Bank of England, to see what happened. At the door was this placard,—"Applicants for dividends will file a written application, with name and amount, at desk A, and proceed in turn to the Paying Teller's Office." I saw their ingenuity. They were making out new books, certain that none would apply but those who were accustomed to. So skilfully do men of Government study human nature.

I stepped lightly to one of the public desks. I took one of the blanks. I filled it out, "John Blatchford, £1747 6*s.* 8*d.*," and handed it in at the open trap. I took my place in the queue in the teller's room. After an agreeable hour, a pile, not thick, of Bank of England notes was given to me; and since that day I have quarterly drawn that amount from the maternal government of that country. As I left the teller's room, I observed the captain in the queue. He was the seventh man from the window, and I have never seen him more.

We then asked Hosanna for her story.

THE N. E. HISTORICAL GENEALOGIST'S STORY.

"My story," said she, "will take us far back into the past. It will be necessary for me to dwell on some incidents in the first settlement of this country, and I propose that we first prepare and enjoy the Christmas-tree. After this, if your courage holds, you shall hear an over-true tale." Pretty creature, how little she knew what was before us!

As we had sat listening to the stories, we had been preparing for the tree. Shopping being out of the question, we were fain from our own stores to make up our presents, while the women were arranging nuts, and blown egg-shells, and pop-corn strings from the stores of the "Eagle and Star." The popping of corn in two corn-poppers had gone on through the whole of the story-telling. All being so nearly ready, I called the drowsy boy again, and, showing him a very large stick in the wood-box, asked him to bring me a hatchet. To my great joy he brought the axe of the establishment, and I bade him farewell. How little did he think what was before him! So soon as he had gone I went stealthily down the stairs, and stepping out into the deep snow, in front of the hotel, looked up into the lovely night. The storm had ceased, and I could see far back into the heavens. In the still evening my strokes might have been heard far and wide, as I cut down one of the two pretty Norways that shaded Mr. Pynchon's front walk, next the hotel. I dragged it over the snow. Blatchford and Steele lowered sheets to me from the large parlor window, which I attached to the larger end of the tree. With infinite difficulty they hauled it in. I joined them in the parlor, and soon we had as stately a tree growing there as was in any home of joy that night in the river counties.

With swift fingers did our wives adorn it. I should have said above, that we travelled with our wives, and that I would recommend that custom to others. It was impossible, under the circumstances, to maintain much secrecy; but it had been agreed that all who wished to turn their backs to the circle, in the preparation of presents, might do so without offence to the others. As the presents were wrapped, one by one, in paper of different colors, they were marked with the names of giver and receiver, and placed in a large clothes-basket. At last all was done. I had wrapped up my knife, my pencil-case, my letter-case, for Steele, Blatchford, and Dick. To my wife I gave my gold watch-key, which fortunately fits her watch; to Hosanna, a mere trifle, a seal ring I wore; to Bertha, my gold chain; and to Sarah Blatchford, the watch which generally hung from it. For a few moments, we retired to our rooms while the pretty Hosanna arranged the forty-nine presents on the tree. Then she clapped her hands, and we rushed in. What a wondrous sight! What a shout of infantine laughter and charming prattle! for in that happy moment were we not all children again?

I see my story hurries to its close. Dick, who is the tallest, mounted a stepladder, and called us by name to receive our presents. I had a nice gold watch-key from Hosanna, a knife from Steele, a letter-case from Phebe, and a pretty pencil-case from Bertha. Dick had given me his watch-chain, which he knew I fancied; Sarah Blatchford, a little toy of a Geneva watch she wore; and her husband, a handsome seal ring, a present to him from the Czar, I believe; Phebe, that is my wife,—for we were travelling with our wives,—had a pencil-case from Steele, a pretty little letter-case from Dick, a watch-key from me, and a French repeater from Blatchford; Sarah Blatchford gave her the knife she carried, with some bright verses, saying that it was not to cut love; Bertha, a watch-chain; and Hosanna a ring of turquoise and amethysts. The other presents were similar articles, and were received, as they were given, with much tender feeling. But at this moment, as Dick was on the top of the flight of steps, handing down a red apple from the tree, a slight catastrophe occurred.

The first I was conscious of was the angry hiss of steam. In a moment I perceived that the steam-boiler, from which the tavern was warmed, had exploded. The floor beneath us rose, and we were driven with it through the ceiling and the rooms above,—through an opening in the roof into the still night. Around us in the air were flying all the other contents and occupants of the Star and Eagle. How bitterly was I reminded of Dick's flight from the railroad track of the Ithaca & Owego Railroad! But I could not hope such an escape as his. Still my flight was in a parabola; and, in a period not longer than it has taken to describe it, I was thrown senseless, at last, into a deep snow-bank near the United States Arsenal.

Tender hands lifted me and assuaged me. Tender teams carried me to the City Hospital. Tender eyes brooded over me. Tender science cared for me. It proved necessary, before I recovered, to amputate my two legs at the hips. My right arm was wholly removed, by a delicate and curious operation, from the socket. We saved the stump of my left arm, which was amputated just below the shoulder. I am still in the hospital to recruit my strength. The doctor does not like to have me occupy my mind at all; but he says there is no harm in my compiling my memoirs, or writing magazine stories. My faithful nurse has laid me on my breast on a pillow, has put a camel's-hair pencil in my mouth, and, feeling almost personally acquainted with John Carter, the artist, I have written out for you, in his method, the story of my last Christmas.

I am sorry to say that the others have never been found.

THE SAME CHRISTMAS IN OLD ENGLAND AND NEW.

THE first Christmas in New England was celebrated by some people who tried as hard as they could not to celebrate it at all. But looking back on that year 1620, the first year when Christmas was celebrated in New England, I cannot find that anybody got up a better *fête* than did these Lincolnshire weavers and ploughmen who had got a little taste of Dutch firmness, and resolved on that particular day, that, whatever else happened to them, they would not celebrate Christmas at all.

Here is the story as William Bradford tells it:

"Ye 16. *day* ye winde came faire, and they arrived safe in this harbor. And after wards tooke better view of ye place, and resolved wher to pitch their dwelling; and ye 25. *day* begane to erecte ye first house for comone use to receive them and their goods."

You see, dear reader, that when on any 21st or 22d of December you give the children parched corn, and let them pull candy and swim candles in nut-shells in honor of the "landing of the Forefathers"—if by good luck you be of Yankee blood, and do either of these praiseworthy things—you are not celebrating the anniversary of the day when the women and children landed, wrapped up in water-proofs, with the dog and John Carver in headpiece, and morion, as you have seen in many pictures. That all came afterward. Be cool and self-possessed, and I will guide you through the whole chronology safely—Old Style and New Style, first landing and second landing, Sabbaths and Sundays, Carver's landing and Mary Chilton's landing, so that you shall know as much as if you had fifteen ancestors, a cradle, a tankard, and an oak chest in the Mayflower, and you shall come out safely and happily at the first Christmas day.

Know then, that when the poor Mayflower at last got across the Atlantic, Massachusetts stretched out her right arm to welcome her, and she came to anchor as early as the 11th of November in Provincetown Harbor. This was the day when the compact of the cabin of the Mayflower was signed, when the fiction of the "social compact" was first made real. Here they fitted their shallop, and in this shallop, on the sixth of December, ten of the Pilgrims and six of the ship's crew sailed on their exploration. They came into Plymouth harbor on the tenth, rested on Watson's island on the eleventh,—which was Sunday,—and on Monday, the twelfth, landed on the mainland, stepping on Plymouth rock and marching inland to explore the country. Add now nine days to this date for the difference then existing between Old Style and New Style, and you come upon the twenty-first of December, which is the day you ought to celebrate as Forefathers' Day. On that day give the children parched corn in token of the new provant, the English walnut in token of the old, and send them to bed with Elder Brewster's name, Mary Chilton's, Edward Winslow's, and John Billington's, to dream upon. Observe still that only these ten men have landed. All the women and children and the other men are over in Provincetown harbor. These ten, liking the country well enough, go across the bay to Provincetown where they find poor Bradford's wife drowned in their absence, and bring the ship across into Plymouth harbor on the sixteenth. Now you will say of course that they were so glad to get here that they began to build at once; but you are entirely mistaken, for they did not do any such thing. There was a little of the John Bull about them and a little of the Dutchman. The seventeenth was Sunday. Of course they could not build a city on Sunday. Monday they explored, and Tuesday they explored more. Wednesday,

"After we had called on God for direction, we came to this resolution, to go presently ashore again, and to take a better view of two places, which we thought most fitting for us; for we could not now take time for further search or consideration, our victuals being much spent, especially our beer."

Observe, this is the Pilgrims' or Forefathers' beer, and not the beer of the ship, of which there was still some store. Acting on this resolution they went ashore again, and concluded by "most voices" to build Plymouth where Plymouth now is. One recommendation seems to have been that there was a good deal of land already clear. But this brought with it the counter difficulty that they had to go half a quarter of a mile for their wood. So there they left twenty people on shore, resolving the next day to come and build their houses. But the next day it stormed, and the people on shore had to come back to the ship, and Richard Britteridge died. And Friday it stormed so that they could not land, and the people on the shallop who had gone ashore the day before could not get back to the ship. Saturday was the twenty-third, as they counted, and some of them got ashore and cut timber and carried it to be ready for building. But they reserved their forces still, and Sunday, the twenty-fourth, no one worked of course. So that when Christmas day came, the day which every man, woman and child of them had been trained to regard as a holy day—as a day specially given to festivity and specially exempted from work, all who could went on shore and joined those who had landed already. So that William Bradford was able to close the first book of his history by saying: "Ye 25. *day* begane to erect ye first house for comone use to receive them and their goods."

Now, this all may have been accidental. I do not say it was not. But when I come to the record of Christmas for next year and find that Bradford writes: "One ye day called Chrismas-day, ye Gov'r caled them out to worke (as was used)," I cannot help thinking that the leaders had a grim feeling of satisfaction in "secularizing" the first Christmas as thoroughly as they did. They wouldn't work on Sunday, and they would work on Christmas.

They did their best to desecrate Christmas, and they did it by laying one of the cornerstones of an empire.

Now, if the reader wants to imagine the scene,—the Christmas celebration or the Christmas desecration, he shall call it which he will, according as he is Roman or Puritan himself,—I cannot give him much material to spin his thread from. Here is the little story in the language of the time:

"Munday the 25. day, we went on shore, some to fell tymber, some to saw, some to riue, and some to carry, so no man rested all that day, but towards night some as they were at worke, heard a noyse of some Indians, which caused vs all to goe to our Muskets, but we heard no further, so we came aboord againe, and left some twentie to keepe the court of gard; that night we had a sore storme of winde and rayne.

"Munday the 25. being Christmas day, we began to drinke water aboord, but at night the Master caused vs to have some Beere, and so on board we had diverse times now and then some Beere, but on shore none at all."

There is the story as it is told by the only man who chose to write it down. Let us not at this moment go into an excursus to inquire who he was and who he was not. Only diligent investigation has shown beside that this first house was about twenty feet square, and that it was for their common use to receive them and their goods. The tradition says that it was on the south side of what is now Leyden street, near the declivity of the hill. What it was, I think no one pretends to say absolutely. I am of the mind of a dear friend of mine, who used to say that, in the hardships of those first struggles, these old forefathers of ours, as they gathered round the fires (which they did have—no Christian Registers for them to warm their cold hands by), used to pledge themselves to each other in solemn vows that they would leave to posterity no detail of the method of their lives. Posterity should not make pictures out of them, or, if it did, should make wrong ones; which accordingly, posterity has done. What was the nature, then, of this twenty-foot-square store-house, in which, afterward, they used to sleep pretty compactly, no man can say. Dr. Young suggests a log cabin, but I do not believe that the log cabin was yet invented. I think it is more likely that the Englishmen rigged their two-handled saws,— after the fashion known to readers of Sanford and Merton in an after age,—and made plank for themselves. The material for imagination, as far as costume goes, may be got from the back of a fifty-dollar national bank-note, which the well-endowed reader will please take from his pocket, or from a roll of Lorillard's tobacco at his side, on which he will find the good reduction of Weir's admirable picture of the embarkation. Or, if the reader has been unsuccessful in his investment in Lorillard, he will find upon the back of the one-dollar bank-note a reduced copy of the fresco of the "Landing" in the Capitol, which will answer his purpose equally well. Forty or fifty Englishmen, in hats and doublets and hose of that fashion, with those odd English axes that you may see in your Æsop's fable illustrations, and with their double-handled saws, with a few beetles, and store of wedges, must make up your tableau, dear reader. Make it *vivant*, if you can.

To help myself in the matter, I sometimes group them on the bank there just above the brook,—you can see the place to-day, if it will do you any good—at some moment when the women have come ashore to see how the work goes on—and remembering that Mrs. Hemans says "they sang"—I throw the women all in a chorus of soprano and contralto voices on the left, Mrs. Winslow and Mrs. Carver at their head, Mrs. W. as *prima assoluta soprano* and Mrs. Carver as *prima assoluta contralto*,—I range on the right the men with W. Bradford and W. Brewster as leaders—and between, facing us, the audience,—who are lower down in the valley of the brook, I place Giovanni Carver (tenor) and Odoardo Winslow (basso) and have them sing in the English dialect of their day,

Suoni la tromba,

Carver waving the red-cross flag of England, and Winslow swinging a broadaxe above his head in similar revolutions. The last time I saw any Puritans doing this at the opera, one had a star-spangled banner and the other an Italian tricolor,—but I am sure my placing on the stage is more accurate than that. But I find it very hard to satisfy myself that this is the correct idealization. Yet Mrs. Hemans says the songs were "songs of lofty cheer," which precisely describes the duet in Puritani.

It would be an immense satisfaction, if by palimpsest under some old cash-book of that century, or by letters dug out from some family collection in England, one could just discover that "John Billington, having become weary with cutting down a small fir-tree which had been allotted to him, took his snaphance and shot with him, and calling a dog he had, to whom in the Low Countries the name Crab had been given, went after fowle. Crossing the brook and climbing up the bank to an open place which was there, he found what had been left by the savages of one of their gardens,—and on the ground, picking at the stalkes of the corne, a flocke of large blacke birds such as he had never seen before. His dogge ran at them and frightened them, and they all took wing heavily, but not so quick but that Billington let fly at them and brought two of them down,—one quite dead and one hurt so badly that he could not fly. Billington killed them both and tyed them together, and following after the flocke had another shot at them, and by a good Providence hurte three more. He tyed two of these together and brought the smallest back to us, not knowing what he brought, being but a poor man and ignorant. Hee is but a lazy Fellowe, and was sore tired with the weight of his burden, which was nigh fortie pounds. Soe soon as he saw it, the Governour and the rest knew that it was a wild Turkie, and albeit he chid Billington sharply, he sent four men with him, as it were Calebs and Joshuas, to bring in these firstlings of the land. They found the two first and brought them to us; but after a long search they could not find the others, and soe gave them up, saying the wolves must have eaten them. There were some that thought John Billington had never seen them either, but had shot them with a long bowe. Be this as it may, Mistress Winslow and the other women stripped them they had, cleaned them, spytted them, basted them, and roasted them, and thus we had fresh foule to our dinner."

I say it would have been very pleasant to have found this in some palimpsest, but if it is in the palimpsest, it has not yet been found. As the Arab proverb says, "There is news, but it has not yet come."

I have failed, in just the same way, to find a letter from that rosy-cheeked little child you see in Sargent's picture, looking out of her great wondering eyes, under her warm hood, into the desert. I overhauled a good many of the Cotton manuscripts in the British Museum (Otho and Caligula, if anybody else wants to look), and Mr. Sainsbury let me look through all the portfolios I wanted in the State Paper Office, and I am sure the letter was not there then. If anybody has found it, it has been found since I was there. If it ever is found, I should like to have it contain the following statement:—

"We got tired of playing by the fire, and so some of us ran down to the brook, and walked till we could find a place to cross it; and so came up to a meadow as large as the common place in Leyden. There was a good deal of ice upon it in some places, but in some places behind, where there were bushes, we found good store of berries growing on the ground. I filled my apron, and William took off his jerkin and made a bag of it, and we all filled it to carry up to the fire. But they were so sour, that they puckered our mouths sadly. But my mother said they were cranberries, but not like your cranberries in Lincolnshire. And, having some honey in one of the logs the men cut down, she boiled the cranberries and the honey together, and after it was cold we had it with our dinner. And besides, there were some great pompions which the men had brought with them from the first place we landed at, which were not like Cinderella's, but had long tails to them, and of these my mother and Mrs. Brewster and Mrs. Warren, made pies for dinner. We found afterwards that the Indians called these pompions, *askuta squash*."

But this letter, I am sorry to say, has not yet been found.

Whether they had roast turkey for Christmas I do not know. I do know, thanks to the recent discovery of the old Bradford manuscript, that they did have roast turkey at their first Thanksgiving. The veritable history, like so much more of it, alas! is the history of what they had not, instead of the history of what they had. Not only did they work on the day when all their countrymen played, but they had only water to drink on the day when all their countrymen drank beer. This deprivation of beer is a trial spoken of more than once; and, as lately as 1824, Mr. Everett, in his Pilgrim oration, brought it in high up in the climax of the catalogue of their hardships. How many of us in our school declamations have stood on one leg, as bidden in "Lovell's Speaker," raised the hand of the other side to an angle of forty-five degrees, as also bidden, and repeated, as also bidden, not to say compelled, the words, "I see them, escaped from these perils, pursuing their almost desperate undertaking, and landed at last, after a five-months' passage, on the ice-clad rocks of Plymouth, weak and exhausted from the voyage, poorly armed, scantily provisioned, depending on the charity of their ship-master for a draught of beer on board, drinking nothing but water on shore, without shelter, without means, surrounded by hostile tribes."

Little did these men of 1620 think that the time would come when ships would go round the world without a can of beer on board; that armies would fight through years of war without a ration of beer or of spirit, and that the builders of the Lawrences and Vinelands, the pioneer towns of a new Christian civilization, would put the condition into the title-deeds of their property that nothing should be sold there which could intoxicate the buyer. Poor fellows! they missed the beer, I am afraid, more than they did the play at Christmas; and as they had not yet learned how good water is for a steady drink, the carnal mind almost rejoices that when they got on board that Christmas night, the curmudgeon ship-master, warmed up by his Christmas jollifications, for he had no scruples, treated to beer all round, as the reader has seen. With that tankard of beer—as those who went on board filled it, passed it, and refilled it—ends the history of the first Christmas in New England.

It is a very short story, and yet it is the longest history of that Christmas that I have been able to find. I wanted to compare this celebration of Christmas, grimly intended for its desecration, with some of the celebrations which were got up with painstaking intention. But, alas, pageants leave little history, after the lights have smoked out, and the hangings have been taken away. Leaving, for the moment, King James's Christmas and Englishmen, I thought it would be a pleasant thing to study the contrast of a Christmas in the countries where they say Christmas has its most enthusiastic welcome. So I studied up the war in the Palatinate,—I went into the chronicles of Spain, where I thought they would take pains about Christmas,—I tried what the men of "la religion," the Huguenots, were doing at Rochelle, where a great assembly was gathering. But Christmas day would not appear in memoirs or annals. I tried Rome and the Pope, but he was dying, like the King of Spain, and had not, I think, much heart for pageantry. I looked in at Vienna, where they had all been terribly frightened by Bethlem Gabor, who was a great Transylvanian prince of those days, a sort of successful Kossuth, giving much hope to beleaguered Protestants farther west, who, I believe, thought for a time that he was some sort of seal or trumpet, which, however, he did not prove to be. At this moment of time he was retreating I am afraid, and at all events did not set his historiographer to work describing his Christmas festivities.

Passing by Bethlem Gabor then, and the rest, from mere failure of their chronicles to make note of this Christmas as it passed, I returned to France in my quest. Louis XIII. was at this time reigning with the assistance of Luynes, the short-lived favorite who preceded Richelieu. Or it would, perhaps, be more proper to say that Luynes was reigning under the name of Louis XIII. Louis XIII. had been spending the year in great activity, deceiving, thwarting, and undoing the Protestants of France. He had made a rapid march into their country, and had spread terror before him. He had had mass celebrated in Navarreux, where it had not been seen or heard in fifty years. With Bethlem Gabor in the ablative,—with the Palatinate quite in the vocative,—these poor Huguenots here outwitted and outgeneralled, and Brewster and Carver freezing out there in America, the Reformed Religion seems in a bad way to one looking at that Christmas. From his triumphal and almost bloodless campaign, King Louis returns to Paris, "and there," says Bassompierre, "he celebrated the *fêtes* this Christmas." So I thought I was going to find in the memoirs of some gentleman at court, or unoccupied mistress of the robes, an account of what the most Christian King was doing, while the blisters were forming on John Carver's hands, and while John Billington was, or was not, shooting wild turkeys on that eventful Christmas day.

But I reckoned without my king. For this is all a mistake, and whatever else is certain, it seems to be certain that King Louis XIII. did not keep either Christmas in Paris, either the Christmas of the Old Style, or that of the New. Such, alas, is history, dear friend! When you read in to-night's "Evening Post" that your friend Dalrymple is appointed Minister to Russia, where he has been so anxious to go, do not suppose he will make you his Secretary of Legation. Alas! no; for you will read in to-morrow's "Times" that it was all a mistake of the telegraph, and that the dispatch should have read "O'Shaughnessy," where the dispatch looked like "Dalrymple." So here, as I whetted my pencil, wetted my lips, and drove the attentive librarian at the Astor almost frantic as I sent him up stairs for you five times more, it proved that Louis XIII. did not spend Christmas in Paris, but that Bassompierre, who said so, was a vile deceiver. Here is the truth in the *Mercure Française,*—flattering and obsequious Annual Register of those days:

"The King at the end of this year, visited the frontiers of Picardy. In this whole journey, which lasted from the 14th of December to the 12th of January (New Style), the weather was bad, and those in his Majesty's suite found the roads bad." Change the style back to the way our Puritans counted it, and observe that on the same days, the 5th of December to the 3d of January, Old Style, those in the suite of John Carver found the weather bad and the roads worse. Let us devoutly hope that his most Christian Majesty did not find the roads as bad as his suite did.

"And the King," continues the *Mercure*, "sent an extraordinary Ambassador to the King of Great Britain, at London, the Marshal Cadenet" (brother of the favorite Luynes). "He departed from Calais on Friday, the first day of January, very well accompanied by *noblesse*. He arrived at Dover the same evening, and did not depart from Dover until the Monday after."

Be pleased to note, dear reader, that this Monday, when this Ambassador of a most Christian King departs from Dover, is on Monday the 25th day of December, of Old Style, or Protestant Style, when John Carver is learning wood-cutting, by way of encouraging the others. Let us leave the King of France to his bad roads, and follow the fortunes of the favorite's brother, for we must study an English Christmas after all. We have seen the Christmas holidays of men who had hard times for the reward of their faith in the Star of Bethlehem. Let us try the fortunes of the most Christian King's people, as they keep their second Christmas of the year among a Protestant people. Observe that a week after their own Christmas of New Style, they land in Old Style England, where Christmas has not yet begun. Here is the *Mercure Français's* account of the Christmas holidays,—flattering and obsequious, as I said:

"Marshal Cadenet did not depart from Dover till the Monday after" (Christmas day, O. S.). "The English Master of Ceremonies had sent twenty carriages and three hundred horses for his suite." (If only we could have ten of the worst of them at Plymouth! They would have drawn our logs for us that half quarter of a mile. But we were not born in the purple!) "He slept at Canterbury, where the Grand Seneschal of England, well accompanied by English noblemen, received him on the part of the King of England. Wherever he passed, the officers of the cities made addresses to him, and offers, even ordering their own archers to march before him and guard his lodgings. When he came to Gravesend, the Earl of Arundel visited him on the part of the King, and led him to the Royal barge. His whole suite entered into twenty-five other barges, painted, hung with tapestry, and well adorned" (think of our poor, rusty shallop there in Plymouth bay), "in which, ascending the Thames, they arrived in London Friday the 29th December" (January 8th, N. S.). "On disembarking, the Ambassador was led by the Earl of Arundel to the palace of the late Queen, which had been superbly and magnificently arranged for him. The day was spent in visits on the part of his Majesty the King of Great Britain, of the Prince of Wales, his son, and of the ambassadors of kings and princes, residing in London." So splendidly was he entertained, that they write that on the day of his reception he had four tables, with fifty covers each, and that the Duke of Lennox, Grand Master of England, served them with magnificent order.

"The following Sunday" (which we could not spend on shore), "he was conducted to an audience by the Marquis of Buckingham," (for shame, Jamie! an audience on Sunday! what would John Knox have said to that!) "where the French and English nobility were dressed as for a great feast day. The whole audience was conducted with great respect, honor, and ceremony. The same evening, the King of Great Britain sent for the Marshal by the Marquis of Buckingham and the Duke of Lennox; and his Majesty and the Ambassador remained alone for more than two hours, without any third person hearing what they said. The following days were all receptions, banquets, visits, and hunting-parties, till the embassy departed."

That is the way history gets written by a flattering and obsequious court editor or organ at the time. That is the way, then, that the dread sovereign of John Carver and Edward Winslow spent his Christmas holidays, while they were spending theirs in beginning for him an empire. Dear old William Brewster used to be a servant of Davison's in the days of good Queen Bess. As he blows his fingers there in the twenty-foot storehouse before it is roofed, does he tell the rest sometimes of the old wassail at court, and the Christmas when the Earl of Southampton brought Will. Shakespeare in? Perhaps those things are too gay,—at all events, we have as much fuel here as they have at St. James's.

Of this precious embassy, dear reader, there is not a word, I think, in Hume, or Lingard, or the "Pictorial"—still less, if possible, in the abridgments. Would you like, perhaps, after this truly elegant account thus given by a court editor, to look behind the canvas and see the rough ends of the worsted? I always like to. It helps me to understand my morning "Advertiser" or my "Evening Post," as I read the editorial history of to-day. If you please, we will begin in the Domestic State Papers of England, which the good sense of somebody, I believe kind Sir Francis Palgrave, has had opened for you and me and the rest of us.

Here is the first notice of the embassy:

Dec. 13. Letter from Sir Robert Naunton to Sir George Calvert.... "The King of France is expected at Calais. The Marshal of Cadenet is to be sent over to calumniate those of the religion (that is, the Protestants), and to propose Madme. Henriette for the Prince."

So they knew, it seems, ten days before we started, what we were coming for.

Dec. 22. John Chamberlain to Sir Dudley Carleton. "In spite of penury, there is to be a masque at Court this Christmas. The King is coming in from Theobalds to receive the French Ambassador, Marshal Cadenet, who comes with a suite of 400 or 500."

What was this masque? Could not Mr. Payne Collier find up the libretto, perhaps? Was it Faith, Valor, Hope, and Love, founding a kingdom, perhaps? Faith with a broadaxe, Valor and Hope with a two-handled saw, while Love dug post-holes and set up timbers? Or was it a less appropriate masque of King James' devising?

Dec. 25. This is our day. Francis Willisfourd, Governor of Dover Castle to Lord Zouch, Warden of the Cinque Ports. "A French Ambassador has landed with a great train. I have not fired a salute, having no instructions, and declined showing them the fortress. They are entertained as well as the town can afford."

Observe, we are a little surly. We do not like the French King very well, our own King's daughter being in such straits yonder in the Palatinate. What do these Papists here?

That is the only letter written on Christmas day in the English "Domestic Archives" for that year! Christmas is for frolic here, not for letter-writing, nor house-building, if one's houses be only built already!

But on the 27th, Wednesday, "Lord Arundel has gone to meet the French Ambassador at Gravesend." And a very pretty time it seems they had at Gravesend, when you look on the back of the embroidery. Arundel called on Cadenet at his lodgings, and Cadenet did not meet him till he came to the stair —head of his chamber-door—nor did he accompany him further when he left. But Arundel was even with him the next morning. He appointed his meeting for the return call *in the street*; and when the barges had come up to Somerset House, where the party was to stay, Arundel left the Ambassador, telling him that there were gentlemen who would show him his lodging. The King was so angry that he made Cadenet apologize. Alas for the Court of Governor John Carver on this side,—four days old to-day—if Massasoit should send us an ambassador! *We* shall have to receive him in the street, unless he likes to come into a palace without a roof! But, fortunately, he does not send till we are ready!

The Domestic Archives give another glimpse:

Dec. 30. Thomas Locke to Carleton: "The French Ambassador has arrived at Somerset House with a train so large that some of the seats at Westminster Hall had to be pulled down to make room at their audience." And in letters from the same to the same, of January 7, are accounts of entertainments given to the Ambassador at his first audience (on that Sunday), on the 4th at Parliament House, on the 6th at a masque at Whitehall, where none were allowed below the rank of a Baron—and at Lord Doncaster's entertainment— where "six thousand ounces of gold are set out as a present," says the letter, but this I do not believe. At the Hampton entertainment, and at the masque there were some disputes about precedency, says John Chamberlain in another letter. Dear John Chamberlain, where are there not such disputes? At the masque at Whitehall he says, "a Puritan was flouted and abused, which was thought unseemly, considering the state of the French Protestants." Let the Marshal come over to Gov. John Carver's court and see one of our masques there, if he wants to know about Puritans. "At Lord Doncaster's house the feast cost three thousand pounds, beside three hundred pounds worth of ambergris used in the cooking," nothing about that six thousand ounces of gold. "The Ambassador had a long private interview with the king; it is thought he proposed Mad.

Henriette for the Prince. He left with a present of a rich jewel. He requested liberation of all the imprisoned priests in the three kingdoms, but the answer is not yet given."

By the eleventh of January the embassy had gone, and Thomas Locke says Cadenet "received a round answer about the Protestants." Let us hope it was so, for it was nearly the last, as it was. Thomas Murray writes that he "proposed a match with France,—a confederation against Spanish power, and asked his Majesty to abandon the rebellious princes,—but he refused unless they might have toleration." The Ambassador was followed to Rochester for the debts of some of his train,—but got well home to Paris and New Style.

And so he vanishes from English history.

His king made him Duke of Chaulnes and Peer of France, but his brother, the favorite died soon after, either of a purple fever or of a broken heart, and neither of them need trouble us more.

At the moment the whole embassy seemed a failure in England,—and so it is spoken of by all the English writers of the time whom I have seen. "There is a flaunting French Ambassador come over lately," says Howel, "and I believe his errand is naught else but compliment.... He had an audience two days since, where he, with his train of ruffling long-haired Monsieurs, carried himself in such a light garb, that after the audience the king asked my Lord Keeper Bacon what he thought of the French Ambassador. He answered, that he was a tall, proper man. 'Aye,' his Majesty replied, 'but what think you of his head-piece? Is he a proper man for the office of an ambassador?' 'Sir,' said Bacon, 'tall men are like houses of four or five stories, wherein commonly the uppermost room is worst furnished.'"

Hard, this, on us poor six-footers. One need not turn to the biography after this, to guess that the philosopher was five feet four.

I think there was a breeze, and a cold one, all the time, between the embassy and the English courtiers. I could tell you a good many stories to show this, but I would give them all for one anecdote of what Edward Winslow said to Madam Carver on Christmas evening. They thought it all naught because they did not know what would come of it. We do know.

And I wish you to observe, all the time, beloved reader, whom I press to my heart for your steadiness in perusing so far, and to whom I would give a jewel had I one worthy to give, in token of my consideration (how you would like a Royalston beryl or an Attleboro topaz).[A] I wish you to observe, I say, that on the Christmas tide, when the Forefathers began New England, Charles and Henrietta were first proposed to each other for that fatal union. Charles, who was to be Charles the First, and Henrietta, who was to be mother of Charles the Second, and James the Second. So this was the time, when were first proposed all the precious intrigues and devisings, which led to Charles the Second, James the Second, James the Third, so called, and our poor friend the Pretender. Civil War—Revolution—1715—1745—Preston-Pans, Falkirk and Culloden—all are in the dispatches Cadenet carries ashore at Dover, while we are hewing our timbers at the side of the brook at Plymouth, and making our contribution to Protestant America.

On the one side Christmas is celebrated by fifty outcasts chopping wood for their fires—and out of the celebration springs an empire. On the other side it is celebrated by the *noblesse* of two nations and the pomp of two courts. And out of the celebration spring two civil wars, the execution of one king and the exile of another, the downfall twice repeated of the royal house, which came to the English throne under fairer auspices than ever. The whole as we look at it is the tale of ruin. Those are the only two Christmas celebrations of that year that I have found anywhere written down!

You will not misunderstand the moral, dear reader, if, indeed, you exist; if at this point there be any reader beside him who corrects the proof! Sublime thought of the solemn silence in which these words may be spoken! You will not misunderstand the moral. It is not that it is better to work on Christmas than to play. It is not that masques turn out ill, and that those who will not celebrate the great anniversaries turn out well. God forbid!

It is that these men builded better than they knew, because they did with all their heart and all their soul the best thing that they knew. They loved Christ and feared God, and on Christmas day did their best to express the love and the fear. And King James and Cadenet,—did they love Christ and fear God? I do not know. But I do not believe, nor do you, that the masque of the one, or the embassy of the other, expressed the love, or the hope, or the faith of either!

So it was that John Carver and his men, trying to avoid the celebration of the day, built better than they knew indeed, and, in their faith, laid a corner-stone for an empire.

And James and Cadenet trying to serve themselves—forgetful of the spirit of the day, as they pretended to honor it—were so successful that they destroyed a dynasty.

There is moral enough for our truer Christmas holidays as 1867 leads in the new-born sister.